G. Keller

Roach Girl origin trilogy three

G. Keller

Mileyjackmedia,
Orlando, Florida

G. Keller

Roach Girl origin trilogy three

Mileyjackmedia, LLC

Orlando, Florida

Copyright © 2024 by G.Keller

ISBN 979-8-9994287-2-1

Cover Art by Janelle Bell-Martin

Roach Girl origin trilogy three

To dad, who taught me perseverance.

G. Keller

"Each relationship between two persons is absolutely unique. That is why you cannot love two people the same. It simply is not possible. You love each person differently because of who they are and the uniqueness that they draw out of you." W. *Paul Young*

G. Keller

Chapter One

Mom came home from the hospital in a wheelchair.

Without a voice.

Without part of her memory.

She knew dad and me, but what happened with Conrad McCormick seemed blocked from her mind.

She could barely walk, barely talk, and barely remember.

She was a visual reminder of what a scumbag McCormick was. No, scumbag was too nice. He was a monster. A criminal. How anyone could escape punishment for what he did, showed me that money, insane amounts of money, ruled. Money was king. If you were loaded, you could get away with anything in life, even attempted murder.

And as mad as I was at McCormick for what he did, I couldn't help but be mad at mom, too. I tried not to be. I was trying so hard to forgive her. I knew she was in a wheelchair and almost died, and may never be the same, but her greed led her to this mess. Money led her to this mess.

Dad tried to explain his part in her departure to me. That it wasn't all mom's fault. That his addiction was too much for anyone to bear. But I beared it. I didn't run away. And she could have stayed, too. She could have hung in there a little bit longer. She could have tried other ways to get dad help. She could have stayed for me. To help *me*. Instead, she had taken the easy way out. She let money manipulate her emotions, her actions, her decisions. Mom being in a wheelchair wasn't just a visual reminder of what McCormick did, it was also a reminder of what mom did. And that was almost worse.

I would never do what she did. Ever. I would never leave my husband or my child because life got tough. So what if we ran out of money. So what if our house wasn't remodeled. So what if you couldn't buy fancy clothes. Why did all of that matter so much? Why did living in the right neighborhood, driving the right car, wearing the right clothes matter so much to some people? Like mom. I didn't get it.

I hated money. Money was evil. Money manipulated people's minds. Money was McCormick. Money was Mom leaving me. Money was a monster.

Now, Dad has to take care of Mom. After leaving him for another man. A rich man.

Yes, I hated money now more than ever before.

Conrad McCormick lured my mother into his sick world with his luxurious lifestyle, and I planned on making him pay for what he did. And maybe then, I could forgive mom for what she did, too.

And my mind could be at peace.

Chapter Two

There was one more week until school started. Conrad McCormick hadn't returned to Portofino since the incident. I figured out how to break into his house on cleaning days. Alarms were off. Maids left doors open. It was easy. Those months I spent alone in Royal Palm Estates, fending for myself by slinking around the fancy neighborhood, scaling the tall rod-iron gate to mom's courtyard entrance, foraging for water, and using bushes for a bathroom, trained me for these missions. For the past month, I had taken expensive dresses, shoes, and handbags mom had purchased when she was with McCormick. I took expensive suits, shoes, and ties from McCormick. I stole all of it without a soul seeing a thing.

Sharon sold them at Sharon's Riches, and we gave half of our profits to Harmony House and the Portofino Homeless Shelter. I told Sharon that mom had given me the clothes. Lying about stealing from the rich to give to the poor left me little remorse.

There was one more thing I did on my Monday break-ins at McCormick's. I left a calling card. I took a jar full of roaches and released them before I left. I had done this every Monday all summer long. The maids were cleaning, and I was releasing tiny German roaches, known to multiply quickly, under the sheets of his huge king-sized bed. The bed he shared with my mom no doubt. I shoved that thought down deep, trying not to think of my mom's part in this. When McCormick finally returned one day, hopefully, he would pull down the bedcovers to hundreds of tiny roaches.

Now, I had one more Monday to steal from him. One more Monday to leave my calling card. One more Monday to try to get even with him. One more Monday before I had to go back to school and stealing from McCormick would get harder to do--no easy entrance. I had to make this Monday count.

I had a routine that worked. Each Monday I rode my bike to his house early in the morning before the maids got there. I hid my bike in the bushes that divided McCormick's mansion and the mansion next door to him. I casually walked across the street to the beach and went for an early morning swim as the sun slowly cast light over the sand and sea.

I swam and swam and swam. The early morning beach was my favorite. The Gulf waters were calm, and I could glide through the salty sea like a dolphin, with effortless power. Stroke. Stroke. Gliiiiiide. Stroke. Stroke. Gliiiiiide. The water renewed and refreshed my skin, my mind, my soul as it rolled like silk over my body. I drifted into a trans-like state. A state of peaceful, quiet euphoria.

After a long, satisfying swim, I toweled off, threw on my t-shirt and shorts, slung my backpack on, and casually walked back to the bushes, waiting for the moment I would slip into his house and hide in the hall closet. But today, when I was crouched down waiting for the right moment to spring into action, a loud noise broke from overhead, descending rapidly out of nowhere. I looked up to see a bright red helicopter looming above like a spaceship ready to zap me up to a foreign planet. I panicked thinking it was the police—on to me at last. I quickly looked towards the street to see if cop cars were racing up to snatch me but saw nothing. Then, in seconds, the helicopter landed on the roof of the mansion next door.

Whew. Close call. A helicopter pad on their roof? Really? The luxurious conveniences of the uber-rich. Why wait on regular air travel when you can just land on your roof? My heart slowed back down. Refocus, Vivian.

I saw my opportunity when a maid went to her van to take a phone call. She leaned on the far side of the hood facing the street. Quickly, I slipped into action, making it to my hiding place in the hall closet, undetected as usual and careful not to touch a thing until deep in the corner where I quickly pulled out my gloves, slipped them on, and gently pulled the door closed. When the other housekeepers' voices drifted to the upstairs rooms, I snuck out and, like a magician, disappeared into the master bedroom closet to find my next treasure.

Clothes were the easiest thing for me to take. There were so many of them. How could anyone know what was missing? No one could. And I easily sold them at Sharon's Riches for ridiculous amounts of money. Money that I gave away to the poor, the vulnerable, the needy.

Mom had left hundreds of designer items, with tags still on, that McCormick couldn't care less about going missing. That's when it hit me. As I gazed at the designer dresses, it hit me so hard I could barely swallow. McCormick couldn't care less that I took these clothes. And I wanted him to care. I wanted him to hurt. I wanted him to pay for what he did, for what money did to my family. I had to steal something bigger. Like the Rolex watches. The grander, the better.

When I sold the Submariner Rolex for $33,300, I felt real revenge. Keeping the Deepsea Rolex was complicated. It was still hidden in my closet. I wasn't sure why I held onto it, but I did and knew I had to get rid of it soon. Having it in my possession was a mixture of anxiety and thrill and power. I had something expensive of his, and weirdly, it made me feel like I had taken some of his power away. Keeping it felt like I was a crusading kidnapper holding materialism captive, waiting for a righteous ransom.

I wanted something like that again. Something that if McCormick found it missing, he would be furious. I wanted that thrill of taking thousands from him to give to the poor. I wanted to make him *really* pay. Stealing clothes for a thousand dollars here and there wasn't satisfying to me anymore. I thirsted for a big heist. Like the watches, only better.

My mind battled between right and wrong. I knew what I was doing was technically wrong. Leo had reminded me of that when I confessed my obsession to him. That 'wrong' drove us apart. Leo represented everything good and pure in life. I loved Leo. I loved him so much I ached to see him, kiss him, touch him, and feel his body against mine. But I drove him away with this uncontrollable need to take from McCormick. He couldn't be with someone like me. A thief. I knew he loved me as much as I loved him, but this vice I was addicted to kept us apart. In my mind, what I was doing wasn't completely wrong. It wasn't. I was giving the money to the poor. Wasn't that a good thing? McCormick had more money than any one human needed. And he was a bad man. Very bad. Why was taking from him to give to the poor wrong?

I needed to try stealing one expensive item. Then, maybe, just maybe, one giant heist could satisfy my thirst for revenge, and I could stop. I could give a giant amount to help the people that were hurt and damaged by ruthless billionaires like McCormick. I could be normal again. Leo would be my boyfriend again. We would swim together, hold hands, kiss. I wanted that back. I longed for Leo's love.

So, I left the closet and wandered out into the hall and just started walking around the house, careful not to get caught by a housekeeper. That wasn't too hard because the house was huge. As I went from room to room, I made my way to a beautiful office with intricate dark molding and bookshelves and leather furniture. I carefully studied the paintings on the walls, too large to steal, but surely expensive originals. Then, looking at the old books on the shelf, I saw the most unique thing leaning on a stand in between stacks of novels. A plate. Not a dinner plate, but about that size. This was a piece of art, and it looked old and somehow familiar. The sketch on it. Abstract. Original, but familiar in some way. I got up close. I gingerly picked it up and turned it over.

Picasso.

I heard a noise and voices getting louder.

My heart raced. I panicked and put it back on its holder.

I needed to leave my calling card. I quickly reached around, unzipped my backpack, and pulled out a jar filled with roaches. I had figured out a way to trap them by putting food in the bottom of the jar in the far corner of our backyard. There were dozens ready to be released. I started to unscrew the lid when voices got louder. Crap. I shoved the jar back in my backpack and hid under the desk. The voices passed by.

I managed to slip out of the house undetected, my heart beating wildly.

I grabbed my bike, flying out of there like a bird taking flight, and soared home. I hadn't taken anything and part of me was furious. I hadn't left the roaches in his bed or his office. I was out of Mondays. School started next week. Why didn't I just steal the plate? Why did I put it back? Stupid.

When I got home, I threw my backpack in the corner and went straight to my computer to look up the value of the Picasso plate.

It didn't take me long. I found the exact plate. Pablo Picasso Madoura Ceramic Plate 'Jacqueline au Chevalet' Ramie 333. Last sold at auction for $60,000 ten years ago.

I turned off the computer. I wanted that plate. It was small and easy to take. I think it could be what I needed to end this desire to steal once and for all. One last satisfying steal to sooth my soul. To satisfy my need for revenge. To satisfy my need to give to the needy, to forgive my mom. Then I could be normal again. Then I could love Leo like he deserved to be loved. Pure. Untainted. Honest. Yes, I needed Leo in my life. This summer without him had been miserable. I wanted him back.

One more time. That is it. Just one more time. Then I won't steal again. I won't.

Chapter Three

I went for my early morning swim every day, looking for an opportunity to break into McCormick's gold mine, thinking maybe the housekeepers would add another day to their cleaning routine. But no. I crept around the outside of his house after my marathon swim the Sunday before school started. We hadn't gone to church since Mom's accident, so I decided to take the morning to try one last time to figure out how to get that Picasso plate. But every door and window were locked. I was going to have to wait. Wait for my opportunity to end this obsession.

Chapter Four

The minute I saw Leo towering above the mass of kids, hair neatly wild, our eyes locked and a thrill shot through my body. I know he felt it, too, because he didn't take his eyes off me and walked straight through the crowd. Without hesitation, he wrapped his limbs around me, and we melted into each other. No one would even know we were no longer dating.

"I missed you," he whispered, and I felt my body flush with instant desire.

"I missed you, too," I murmured.

"Let me see your schedule," he said, pulling back from our embrace. "We have Entrepreneurship together right after lunch. Meet me at our table after fourth period?" he asked hopefully.

I nodded yes.

***

The cafeteria at lunch was buzzing with electric excitement. Old friends catching up. New classes. New teachers. New kids.

"See that new kid over there?" Dexter's head nodded in the direction of a table in the far corner of the cafeteria as he sat down with a tray of food.

We all turned to look, briefly, trying not to be rude.

A kid sat alone.

I did a double take. That kid was in every one of my classes this morning. I remember in homeroom thinking I didn't recognize him. I thought maybe I just didn't have any classes with him last year. But I remember thinking it was odd because Lorenzo was small and by the end of last year, everybody knew everybody. And I had never seen that kid before.

"Yea, what about him?" asked Dushon. Our lunch table had dwindled down to Leo, Dexter, Dushon, and me. Macy and Kendall had graduated and now worked at the Portofino Community Hospital. I was the only girl left in our group. In a way, I liked it. I liked my construction crew. I preferred being one of the boys.

Leo sat down next to me, close. "What's up?"

Dexter continued, "That is ex-Governor Wilson's kid, Wyatt. He has been kicked out of every school in town, public and private. His daddy got him in here. He is a sophomore."

I knew he wasn't here last year. Kids didn't get into Lorenzo after freshman year. The waiting list was so long that it was hard to get in even as a freshman. Lorenzo Williams Technical High School had become the number one Title One high school in Florida and ranked in the top 100 nationally. Seventy-three percent of the student body was on free and reduced lunch. This school was dedicated to getting hard-working students from underprivileged homes a good start in life. Once kids were in, they never left. So, getting into this school as a sophomore was unusual.

All I could think was, 'Of course he got in. Money bends rules. Money gets you into schools that are full with waiting lists. Money gets you off an attempted murder rap. Money makes you leave your husband and kid. Money is king.'

The more I thought about it, the madder I got. There were poor, hard-working kids trying to get into this school and couldn't. Kids who needed scholarships, needed help, whose parents worked two or three jobs to put food on the table. This kid doesn't need a scholarship. He doesn't need any help. How dare he take the spot of a well-deserving student?

"His parties are legendary," Dushon added.

"Like you have ever been to one of his parties," Dexter jabbed and cut up laughing.

"I almost went once," Dushon defended.

"How can they be legendary? The kid is like fifteen. What, has he been having parties since he was twelve?" Dexter continued to jab.

"Well, all I know is for the last year, every kid in Portofino—except us, apparently—have been going to his parties on Friday nights," Dushon informed.

"Should we invite him to sit with us?" Leo asked. "I kind of feel sorry for him sitting alone over there."

"No!" I blurted bluntly.

Everyone looked at me. "Sorry, I didn't mean to sound rude, but I don't want some rich snot over here."

"Uhum. Weren't you the rich snot that we befriended last year?" Leo smirked.

"You know I was far from rich," I looked down, turning dark and defensive.

"Sorry, you were going through a hard time. But you were once rich. We have no idea what he is going through. Kicked out of every school might mean a troubled home life," Leo reasoned. "You came here because things were tough. Cut him some slack."

Leo was right. Again. I was once a rich kid. Country Club Girl. Remember her, Viv? Remember how she lost it all. Had to survive on her own.

"My situation was different. You know that Leo," I was getting upset that he was bringing up such personal stuff. Dexter and Dushon knew everything.

They helped restore our Royal Palm Estates home and knew it all. But still. I didn't want to talk about my painful past. "I doubt the kid of Governor Wilson has it tough. The Wilsons are the richest family in Florida."

The bell was ready to ring, and I was glad to end this conversation and glad I didn't have to make small talk with a rich snot. We all got up to dump our trash when Wyatt walked our way. I looked at him and noticed he was staring at me.

"What are you looking at?" I snapped.

Dushon and Dexter exchanged looks. Leo looked horrified and whispered, "Hey, chill. You sound mean."

My words *were* icy. I knew it but didn't care. This rich kid had no business being here. And there Leo went again, telling me how to act. Pointing out another flaw. First thief. Now let's add mean.

"I know you," Wyatt didn't let my rude comment phase him and didn't break his stare.

"I don't know what you are talking about," I said, toning down my attitude, slightly, but not much.

"I have seen you before," he wouldn't let up.

Leo now turned to me quizzically, skeptically. As if lying was about to be added to his list of flaws about me. I didn't like Leo's look. Like a drippy faucet, Leo's trust for me was leaking out slowly. Self-righteous, perfect Leo. Was that disappointment casting a shadow again?

"The only place you have seen me is in every class today. We have had the exact same schedule all morning," my voice still had an edge.

"No, I recognized you instantly," he cut in front of all of us and dumped his tray and looked right back into my face up close and lowered his voice dominantly. "I know you." Then he turned and walked away.

Dexter, Dushon, and Leo were all staring at me. "I have no idea what he is talking about." And I turned and walked towards period five, Leo next to me, but with greater distance between us.

When entering Entrepreneur class, there he was again, Wyatt Wilson. The nightmare continues. I walked to the furthest table from where the rich snot was seated and plunked my backpack on the table.

Leo whispered, "Why are you acting this way? Be nicer to him. You don't even know him," Leo diplomatically whispered.

I sighed a big, heavy sigh. "I know all I need to know. His dad was governor of Florida, like forever, who owns almost the entire state. He has been kicked out of every school in town, apparently. Probably spoiled rotten and nothing is ever good enough. What is there to really learn?" I stated matter-a-factly.

"Woa, Viv. There is always more to people than you think. Don't believe all the gossip," Leo suggested.

I eased up a second and looked at Leo's beautiful face. His caramel smooth skin, delicate features, and sky-blue eyes naturally radiated gentleness. He seemed to have grown since last year and towered over me more than ever. A gentle giant. He was such an amazing person. I remembered our bodies intertwined on the beach, me wanting more and him holding back, looking at me tenderly. I was in desperate need of love, feeling abandoned by my parents and so scared and alone, yet he didn't take advantage of my vulnerability. He just loved me, respected me, and made me feel whole. Everything about him was good and kind and pure. I melted a little just looking at him. He was right. I needed to stop acting like an ass.

"Ok," I caved. I wasn't going to like him, but I could be polite. "I'll go apologize."

Leo smiled.

The teacher hadn't entered the room yet, so I reluctantly walked over to Wyatt and said, "Sorry about lunch. I was rude."

Wyatt tore a piece of paper from a notebook and wrote down something and folded it in half. "Come to my party Friday night."

"I don't think so. I don't drink," I replied, caught off guard and trying to sound polite. His dark brown eyes, glaring intensely, were fiercely the opposite of Leo's gentle light eyes. His hair was similar to mine, thick, blonde, and wavy. Something about him looked familiar. Had I seen him before? No. I would remember. But there was something familiar.

"Who said you had to drink? Just come," and staring right at me with a slight smartass smirk, he handed me the paper and added, "You know where it is."

I took the paper and opened it.

I felt my face flame.

. Shit.

I walked back to my table with my head down, crumpled the paper, and shoved it into my pocket. I knew Leo was looking at me, and I needed my face to pale up before he saw me. I needed to regain my composure. I finally glanced at Leo's questioning face, but something else caught my eye. Something moved on my backpack which was resting on the table.

A roach. Perched on the zipper, scouting out its next move.

Chapter Five

"What did he give you?" Leo's voice sounded slightly jealous.

"He invited me to one of his 'legendary' parties," I twirled my eyes.

"What did you tell him?"

"I told him I didn't party. Don't worry. I was polite."

The teacher entered the room and began the class. Rescued. Mr. Miller introduced himself and enthusiastically began to explain a big competition that all the Entrepreneur classes from all the high schools in Portofino were participating in this semester called 'Shark Tank.' Each school held a competition to select a team for the county finals. Then the winning county team went to a state competition. The state champions won full scholarships to any state college or university and participated in a national competition held by the real Shark Tank millionaires from the famous TV show. Leo seemed swept up in Mr. Miller's excitement for this project, and he lost interest in my exchange with Wyatt and his party invitation.

But I couldn't shake it. I couldn't shake Wyatt's intense stare. I couldn't shake the address on the piece of paper. I glanced over at Wyatt, and he caught my look. I could feel his eyes on me even though I quickly turned back to Mr. Miller. I felt my face turn red again. Damn. I couldn't shake this feeling that Wyatt Wilson was going to be trouble.

Chapter Six

Leo was a senior and left after period five to work at an internship with a luxury home builder here in town. Leo was super excited about his internship. I knew he wanted to build mansions like the ones in Olde Portofino. He had worked for RG construction, but Dad and Mr. Cooper specialized in remodeling small homes. I knew that wasn't what Leo wanted to do. This company had just demolished a charming cottage a few blocks from the pier and the beach to build a modern castle. I hated it. The house they tore down had history and character. So what if it was small. Who needs 10,000 square feet of space? But I knew Leo loved learning how to build a luxury home. I saw his face when we remodeled my old house in Royal Palm Estates. His eyes lit up when the high-end kitchen cabinets, marble countertops, and fancy light fixtures were installed. Leo knew I wanted nothing to do with that kind of building. I loved how Dad and Mr. Cooper started RG construction, and that they remodeled quaint, charming cottages.

Period six was accounting, and luckily, Wyatt wasn't in that class. One class without him. Thank you, God.

After school let out, I walked home alone, obsessing about the note Wyatt had slipped me. That address. 9198 Blue Dolphin Lane. Chills shot through my body leaving me goose bumps. I had never seen Wyatt Wilson before today. I had never been to one of his parties. We had never gone to the same school or had the same friends.

But I *have* been to 9196 Blue Dolphin Lane, the home of Conrad McCormick.

Chapter Seven

Dad and Mr. Cooper had stopped teaching full-time at LWTHS and developed a work study program where kids learned on-the-job skills like carpentry, electrical, plumbing, painting, and tiling, basically all the trades needed to build a house. So, when I got home, Dad was sitting at the kitchen table with stacks of bills and papers organized in neat piles. He looked stressed, rubbing his temples, mouth tight.

"Everything OK?" I asked.

"Nothing for you to worry about. How was your first day of school?"

"Fine."

Dad had taken me to school today because it was the first day, but starting tomorrow, he would have to leave super early to check on the job sites of two homes he was remodeling. I had asked Leo if he would start picking me up in the morning.

Dad was about to leave again now that I was home. He didn't like leaving mom too long unsupervised. Her memory was getting better daily, but she was still weak and needy and could barely speak.

Doctors were encouraged that she would have a full recovery with a lot of physical therapy but warned us that her voice may never return. Dad got up and grabbed his orange jug of water.

"I'll be home late. Your mother is resting. Just order a pizza for dinner," he kissed me and vanished out the door.

I settled at the table after his departure and looked at the neatly organized stacks. I picked up a paper. A hospital bill. $3,456. I looked at the second paper in the stack. $1,689. The third. $527. The fourth. $12,444. Crap. Dad was stressed about money. Again. Worry always wormed its way into my world. I hated this feeling. Why? Why can't we escape money stress? Everything was so much better after we sold Royal Palm Estates. Dad paid off all our bills and bought this house, and we made it cute. We started RG Construction with the goal of restoring old homes for struggling middle class families and giving part of the profits to charity. Dad didn't make a fortune, but we were comfortable with little stress and the satisfaction of doing something good for people. I picked up a pay stub from LWTHS. The paltry salary he was getting from teaching the work/study program hardly covered our regular bills. He was making money on the remodels, but we kept the prices low enough for people to afford the homes.   Again, my parents were in a money problem. Anger started to simmer. I clenched my fists and closed my eyes, breathing deeply. I tried to keep from exploding, but the anger began to boil. Anger towards McCormick. Anger towards Mom. Anger towards money.

As I sat there staring at our problems organized in neat stacks, chest tight with difficulty breathing, a bean-sized roach scurried across the bills. Just like the roach that was on my backpack at school today. Where were they coming from? Did we have an infestation? Was my trap in the far back corner of the yard luring them to our house? Then I remembered the jar I shoved in the side compartment of my backpack when I was at McCormick's last week. I had forgotten to take it out. As I unzipped the bag and pulled out the jar, I saw the lid had been loose.

The roach hustled down the table leg and scuttled across the floor to the kitchen cabinets. I couldn't have roaches in our kitchen or in our house. I set the jar on the table and grabbed a dish cloth to trap it and wrap it up to release outside. I opened the bottom drawer where it had disappeared and froze. I tried to swallow but couldn't. *No. No. NO!*

There in the bottom drawer was a box of wine. I grabbed it. Empty. It was empty. Damn it dad! *Why? WHY???* I slammed the box into the trashcan.

G. Keller

Chapter Eight

After taking the trash to the can in the garage, I cleaned out my backpack. The jar had three remaining roaches, so I knew many had escaped. Had I left a trail of roaches all over school on my first day? Had kids seen me walking around with roaches crawling out of the seams of my backpack or trailing down my body?

Flashbacks to that fateful day at Beachside Middle, when roaches exploded from my lunch bag, crawled all over me, and sent me fleeing to the media center, entered my mind. How that one event changed my life. How horrible it seemed at the time, but how it led me to Leo and LWTHS. If that humiliating event hadn't happened, I would not have gotten into this school and saved my dad. But I didn't want kids to make fun of me at Lorenzo. I was suddenly paranoid. I emptied out the jar and took the backpack to the laundry room and soaked it in soap.

With images of the roach scene from eighth grade trapped and bouncing around in my head, I suddenly thought, no. The kids at this school were different. I couldn't think of one person who would make fun of me or take pictures of me and post them, trying to degrade me. Not one. That is why I hated Wyatt being at Lorenzo. I hated him bringing that snotty rich kid phoniness into my sweet school.

I switched off the old movie in my mind and switched on the new release. Dad drinking again. Then I rummaged through every drawer, in every cupboard, looking for roaches and boxes of wine. Maybe it was just a small mess-up. Maybe dad just had a little bit, and it was nothing to worry about. Maybe I was making too much out of one small box of wine. But deep down in the pit of my stomach, I knew better.

Damn. Blood drained from my body. There, under the sink behind all the cleaning supplies, was a grocery bag full of never opened wine boxes. Dad *was* drinking again, and not just a little. My heart plummeted. Dad stopped going to church because Mom wasn't able to go yet, and he hadn't gone to any AA meetings either. Dad suddenly had Mom's medical bills to pay. Dad was stressed, and I see now that when dad gets stressed, he turns to wine.

Furious, I jerked the bag out of its hiding place and grabbed a knife. I stabbed the box of wine violently making a giant, jagged hole and then poured the contents down the sink. I stabbed each box until they were all empty and took them out to the trash.

After I found Dad almost dead in the Everglades, and he began to heal with the help of Mr. Cooper and church and AA, I thought my nightmare was ending. And then seeing Dad holding Mom in the hospital, I thought we were putting our family back together again. Like it used to be before buying the mansion in Royal Palm Estates and trying to remodel it. Before Dad lost his medical license for operating on the wrong eye. Before Dad's depression sent him drinking and Mom shopping. Before the bills got so bad my parents buckled, leaving me alone and abandoned.

This can't happen again. It can't. This time instead of lifeless dad, it was lifeless Mom. But how much longer before Dad's drinking sends him to the couch, too? Will both of my parents cave under pressure again? Will they leave me again?

My heart beat like a tribal drum sending a distress signal.

I needed to swim in the Gulf. Now. To quiet the panic. I changed into my suit, threw on shorts and a T-shirt, and slipped into my flip flops. I cracked open mom's door. She slumbered silently. I stopped suddenly and stared at her sleeping. My mind flashed to the moment paramedics pulled her lifeless body from McCormick's mansion. I had been so furious with her for leaving me until I saw her rolling out on a stretcher.

I thought she was dead. In that moment, I crumbled. I loved her so much despite her leaving dad and me.

Now, looking at her laying there in bed, chest silently moving up and down, I was engulfed with conflicting emotions. I loved her deeply. I loved the mom from when I was little. The mom who took me to the beach, shopping, birthday parties, playgrounds, swimming pools. The mom who sang Silent Night to me every night for so many years, even when it wasn't Christmas because that song soothed me to sleep. The mom who taught me to bake brownies, tie my shoes, and jump rope. The happy, young mom who showered me with attention and love.

But part of me hated her, too. I didn't want to hate her, but I did. I hated that she left dad to nearly die. I hated that she left me utterly alone, with no food, water, electricity, or means of support. I hated that she never called me once for over a year to see if I was OK. I hated that she left me, us, for shopping, for money. Would mom even be here if McCormick was a great guy? It was the question lurking around in my head. The question I didn't want to face. The question dad probably battles as he cracks open a box of wine. The truth is, probably not. If McCormick would have loved mom and cared for her and not been the monster he turned out to be, mom would probably still be with him. Let's face facts, Vivian. Mom had a shopping addiction, and if McCormick wouldn't have strangled and beat her to near death, she would probably be strolling through Saks about now instead of here, dumping her medical bills on dad.

I stared at her peaceful face. She looked like Sleeping Beauty lying there. I love you mom, but I hate you, too. I do. I hate that because of your greed, dad is drinking—again. Because of your greed, I am a thief. I am a person I never wanted to be. Damaged. A damaged person. That is what you did to me, mom. Damaged me. I'm an unlovable person who doesn't deserve a great guy like Leo. Because of you, my mind can't rest. Because of you, I need to swim and swim and swim to wash off the shame and drown the anger.

Mom had a notepad and pen laying on her bed for communication next to a large sketchbook for drawing. I opened the small notepad and scribbled that I would only be gone for an hour. Then stopped when I was about to lay it next to her. Why did I care how long I would be? She didn't care when she left me. On second thought, I crumpled up the note and tossed it in the trash on my way out the door. I'll be home when I get home.

I rode my bike to the Pier this time. It wasn't far from McCormick's mansion, but far enough. I wasn't going near that place for a while. Wyatt Wilson had seen me there. I wondered how many times. What had he seen? Did he see me steal? I thought I had been so careful all summer. But obviously not careful enough. I didn't want to swim by Charlotte and Jewel's mansions either because their houses reminded me of such a painful time, and I was trying to rid myself of any emotion. Instead, I went north of the pier where high-rise condos flanked the shoreline. The waves were always a little choppier there and didn't make for easy swimming, but I wanted a hard workout. I wanted the force of the undertow to work against my body. I wanted to push through something rough to feel powerful.

The warm water melted my worry as I sunk into its salty healing powers. I held my breath and just swam and swam and swam. When I finally came up for air, I was a far distance north of the pier. There was a rocky jetty ahead of me that I remember coming to as a small child. My parents would bring me here, and we snorkeled around the jagged rocks on calmer days. There was always some living treasure to find. Tiny crabs, starfish, sand dollars, stingrays, and even a manatee once that nearly scared the heck out of Mom when it slowly emerged out of nowhere.

As I approached the rocks, I longed for those happy days when life seemed so simple. Mom and Dad holding hands, laughing, excited to watch my new sea creature discovery. This was another reason why I loved to swim. It reminded me of moments I cherished, happy family memories. But today I felt lost, lonely, anxious, and the swim wasn't helping those feelings go away. Why did there have to be more bills to pay? Why did dad start drinking again? Why did I feel this uncontrollable urge to steal? Why did stealing give me some sort of euphoric power? Power that kept me from letting Leo love me.

Before swimming back, I let my body drift ashore and plopped on the sand for a while, staring out to sea, thinking. I could go talk to Sharon, but she was marrying Mr. Cooper and was so busy running her store and planning her wedding. The last time I was there she hardly had time for hello. I stopped working at Sharon's Riches because I had to watch mom when dad went to work. We left mom for brief periods, but not more than a few hours. I had taken her some clothes to sell after my Monday stealing ventures, but that was it. I didn't feel like sharing this secret just yet. I didn't want anyone to know Dad was drinking again. Maybe I could fix it before it got out of hand.

The sand began to burn my legs, so I went back into the water and started swimming slowly to where I left my towel and bike near the pier. The waves were strong, so I was getting nowhere. Turning over onto my back, I drifted with the swells of the waves, staring up at the bright blue sky. I was being pushed to shore but didn't really care. What was I going to do about Dad's drinking? How were we going to pay the mounting medical bills?

A pelican glided overhead. I decided that the first thing I would do is get Dad back to AA and church. Church helped heal my dad. He needed God's guidance. And besides, I wanted to see more of Leo outside of school. After seeing him today, I knew I needed his goodness back in my life. Without Leo, my mind wandered wildly into dark places. He kept me honest and good. He was the reason I needed to stop stealing. In fact, his presence in my life made me *want* to stop stealing.

Next, since I was on to Dad's drinking, I planned to hunt down every hiding place, daily, to rid our home of wine. If I kept throwing it away, he would know that I knew and maybe motivate him to stop. I felt a little better making a plan. Rolling over, I swam back to the pier, cutting through the water like a dolphin. When I got close, I angled towards shore, standing when my feet touched the sand.

Oh no. I plunged back into the water. Coming straight towards me was Wyatt Wilson, walking, while holding a surfboard on his head.

Chapter Nine

Why was I suddenly seeing this kid everywhere? It was bad enough that I had five classes with him today. Now he was haunting my happy place.

Plunging quicky underwater, I held my breath and started to kick away in a panic. Tired from my long swim but energized by my nerves, I swam and swam and swam. Out of breath, I finally popped up, gasping. I was way out past the pier. Then, out of nowhere, my foot grazed sand. A sand bar this far out? I crawled up on it and sat, water just waist deep, and regained a little strength. How did I get this far? Waves were picking up power on the far side of the sand bar. I managed to push myself off towards the other side of the pier, away from Wyatt, and eventually coasted to shore. I had lost sight of Wyatt and walked along the shore to retrieve my towel and my bike.

As I began to peddle away, I heard, "Vivian!"

Looking around, I spotted Leo across the street at a construction site. His internship. I biked over to him and said, "Hey."

"What are you doing here?" he asked.

"I just went for a swim."

45

"I saw Wyatt a few minutes ago, on his way to the beach with a surfboard. Did you see him?" Leo asked. There was a concerned look in Leo's eyes. A look I had never seen. Jealousy? Was Leo jealous? Did he think I was secretly meeting Wyatt?

Should I just say no to relieve Leo's sudden doubt? After all, there was no exchange between Wyatt and me. But why would I need to lie? I didn't do anything wrong, so I let the truth tumble out. "Yea, but he didn't see me. I just wanted to swim, so I avoided him."

That seemed to ease the concern from Leo's face, a little. "Well, I better get back to work. See you in the morning?"

"Yea, see you tomorrow." We didn't hug. We didn't kiss. In fact, the exchange felt awkward, like we were acquaintances. The swim was supposed to make me feel better, but as I rode my bike home, I felt uneasy, like life was beginning to unravel…. again.

Chapter Ten

I lay in bed that night unable to sleep, staring at the ceiling. Unpaid bills. Dad drinking. Mom's recovery. McCormick. Leo. Wyatt. When will the worry wane?

My eye lids drooped, and I drifted into a deep dream.... *I am drowning far out to sea. Something is pulling me down. A sea monster with octopus tentacles is wrapping its slimy suction cups around my legs. I try to break free. I pull and pull, but the suction cups are stuck on my skin, and I can't pull them off. Another slimy tentacle wraps around my neck. I feel myself being strangled, unable to breathe. Suddenly, superhuman strength seizes my soul, and I grab a tentacle, ripping it off my neck, and then grab the one on my leg and pull with brut force. I jerk the monster into the air as I break the surface of the water violently, inhale deeply, and begin to swing the octopus around and around with mighty force, like a comic book superhero.*

I fling the creature so far into the air that it flies across the sky, past the pier, past McCormick's mansion, and collides with a red helicopter. The chopper's blades

*slicing the monster into bloody bits, now being spattered
everywhere.*

*I am no longer in the sea, but on a wall, scurrying
frantically this way and that, not knowing which way to
go. I feel weightless, panicked, and invincible at the same
time. Where am I now? I look at my legs and there are
four of them, brown and jagged. My back has light brown
wings, so I take flight, but only manage a short distance
to a brown bookshelf, instinctively camouflaged. In front
of me is a giant plate. The Picasso plate. I lift the plate
and perch it on my back and take off flying and flying and
flying. I hear a scream. Leo. His voice shouts to put it
back. Another scream. Wyatt. His voice shouts to take
it. I fly out the window with the plate on my back and
soar over the Gulf. Looking down, I see sharks, tons of
sharks. I feel the heavy weight of the plate. My
weightless, winged body is sinking out of the sky like a
malfunctioning helicopter. I am trying to regain control
and go higher, away from the teaming sharks below, but
I'm falling closer and closer to the water. I am about to
sink into the sea when I chuck the plate from my back,
and it splashes into the choppy surface, free to flutter and
fly frantically upwards again. Suddenly a great white
shark catapults itself out of the sea like lava spewing from
a volcano. I see its teeth. I'm about to be eaten.*

I jolted awake, sweating and breathing and gasping. Calm down. Calm down. Calm down. Nightmare, Viv. Only a nightmare.

Chapter Eleven

The next morning, I woke up early. Dad was sitting at the table with a cup of coffee going over the stacks of bills and writing stuff down on a pad of paper.

"Dad," I said. He looked up and I continued. "Why don't you just not give anything to charity on your next few home remodels? Then you can pay off Mom's hospital bills."

Dad smiled warmly. "Well, that is a good idea, but the loan for these projects comes from a special Federal Grant requiring me to give to charity. I have no choice on these projects," he hesitated. "But that is OK. I want to give the money. It is the heart and soul of the company. I just need to take on a few more projects. Then we will be fine. Your mother is recovering more and more each day. We will figure out a way to pay the bills. Do not worry."

I wanted to believe him. I did. But I knew the bills were mounting higher and higher. And as I walked to the kitchen sink, I smelled alcohol. I glanced at Dad's coffee mug. That wasn't coffee in it. My chest clenched, suffocating my heart for a few seconds. I took a deep breath, trying to calm my uncertainty.

Chapter Twelve

"Leo, I think we should enter the Shark Tank competition. You haven't gotten a scholarship yet, and I need the scholarship money, too," I said, after I slid into Leo's car. I couldn't stop thinking of all our bills and not wanting to add college tuition to the mix in a couple of years.

"You know, I was thinking the same thing," Leo glanced over to me and reached his hand across the seat taking hold of mine. I knew what he wanted. He wanted us back together. I could see it in his eyes. I saw the jealous look he had when he thought I had gone to the beach to meet Wyatt. He wanted to date again, and I wanted that, too. I loved Leo. I needed Leo. His goodness calmed my soul. But I just wasn't ready. I had too much anger. Too much revenge I needed to release. And now, with Dad drinking and bills mounting, I had to fix another problem before I let Leo into my life. Leo deserved pure, unencumbered love.

After waking up from my bizarre nightmare last night, I couldn't sleep. My mind was brainstorming solutions to our family money problem. I thought the profits from the remodels would work, but when dad said no, I thought of my second idea. McCormick's plate. Maybe my nightmare about the plate was a sign for me to take it. I could sell it and pay off mom's medical bills. After all, McCormick owed more than that to my mother. The money could come from an 'angel donor.' The angel being Roach Girl. Yes, that could work. I needed to take the plate soon and fix this problem. I didn't want dad falling too deep into a drunken depression. Soon. Do it soon. Then Leo and I could be together. Then mom and dad could start over.

I pretended to need something from my backpack, still damp from yesterday's cleansing, and slipped out of Leo's affectionate hand- holding without appearing purposeful. I didn't look at his face to see if he was hurt.

We arrived at school and hugged goodbye. "See you at lunch," he whispered.

"OK," I said, and off I went to chemistry.

When I walked through the classroom door, there were name cards propped on each table. Uhg, a seating chart. I slowed my pace, scanned the room, and searched for my name. Oh no! Wyatt Wilson's name card was right next to mine. I quickly looked at the teacher to see if I could do a switcheroo with another name card, but she was looking right at me. I slunk into the seat with my name.

Seconds later, Wyatt walked casually through the door, his blonde hair and tanned skin brighter from yesterday's surf. He stopped when he saw what was going on. He looked right at me and the card next to me.

"Hey," he said, sliding into the adjacent chair.

"Hey," I repeated, feeling uptight and awkward.

The teacher went over the purpose of the seating chart and that we were working with partners this week. Ugh. I had to talk to Portofino's party-boy all week. The party-boy that had seen me at McCormick's. How much did he know about my Roach Girl escapades?

I am not sure if I was distracted by the uncomfortable feeling I had working with Wyatt, or I just had a brain blockage when it came to chemistry, but I didn't understand a word Mrs. Robbins was saying. Or maybe it was a combination of both, but what I did know was I hated it. I hated chemistry. I hated not understanding. I suddenly felt stupid, especially since Wyatt seemed to be a genius at chemistry. He understood everything with ease, making me feel even more uncomfortable and frustrated. He was supposed to be a pot-head party boy with a mission to get kicked out of schools and live a lavish Portofino lifestyle, surfing, driving luxury cars, boating to the Bahamas, and not caring about anything. His sudden aptitude for science completely caught me off-guard, and I hated it. I hated him being smarter than me at this. I suddenly loathed chemistry and Wyatt's superiority of the subject.

I was relieved when the bell rang and more relieved when I didn't have to sit by him in any of my other classes the rest of the morning. When I got to lunch, I was happy to see Leo.

"Hi," I gave Leo a giant smile and hug.

"Hello," Leo returned the smile and hugged me tighter than usual, responding to my enthusiastic gesture.

Wyatt sat alone, again. I glanced over at him, and his nose was in a book.

After lunch, in Mr. Miller's class, Leo and I paired up to work on an assignment I loved. We were analyzing great marketing campaigns of successful products and businesses. Mr. Miller was teaching us business and marketing strategies for the upcoming Shark Tank competition. Leo and I worked great together. When I was with Leo, I felt comfortable, relaxed, smart, myself.

I wanted to get this McCormick monkey off my back asap. I wanted Leo in my life as a boyfriend. I wanted McCormick to pay for my mom's medical bills that HE caused. I wanted to take that plate this weekend. The compulsion to steal something from McCormick infested every pore in my body.

And as I walked home from school that afternoon, by myself, I hatched the perfect plan.

Chapter Thirteen

That night, I went over the plan in my head until I perfected it. I played it out again and again, brainstorming anything that could go wrong and what I would do if it did. With each rehashing, I grew in confidence that it would work.

Wyatt lived next door to McCormick. Friday night he was having a big party, probably with loud music and hundreds of kids. I would hide my bike in my usual spot in the hedges between the two mansions. I knew exactly where the plate was in McCormick's office. If there was no easy entry, I would wait until the party was at its most obnoxious point and break a window, run in and grab the plate, shove it in my backpack, and race out. Even if an alarm went off, I would either grab my bike and casually ride off, or blend into the party, pretending to be another drunk teen, leaving the police to think some rowdy kids decided to pull a prank.

Once I had the plate, I would take it and the Deepsea Rolex I was keeping, to Roy at the pawnshop, have him list the items for sale online, pay off my mother's medical bills, save some for future bills, and when mom was better, give the rest to charity. I would continue to use mom's ID, and if McCormick tried to track down the plate and found out it was being sold by my mom, I doubt he would pursue pressing charges. After all, he did almost kill my mother. Then, all my problems would be solved, and Leo and I could be together with no baggage hanging over me.

Chapter Fourteen

I was uptight and anxious all week. Every day, I had to deal with Wyatt in chemistry outsmarting me, making me feel dumb. Why couldn't I understand chemistry? I hated feeling inferior to him. And why had he been kicked out of every school in town? He was smart, brilliant actually, and he clearly liked chemistry. It didn't add up.

On the other hand, Leo and I were killing it in Mr. Miller's Entrepreneur class. We rocked every assignment, and I grew in confidence that we had a chance at winning the school's Shark Tank competition.

On Friday, Mr. Miller gave us fictitious products, and we pretended to pitch them to the class, working on our presentation skills. Leo and I were completely in cinq. The class cheered after our presentation, bolstering our confidence. I was running on the adrenaline of knowing that soon I would finally be ridding myself of my dark thoughts. Thoughts of revenge. Thoughts of financial relief. Thoughts of restoring my family. Then, all the pain and bitterness would be released.

Chapter Fifteen

I decided to dress like a kid going to a party at Wyatt Wilson's mansion. The ex-governor's kid. Everyone knows the Wilsons. Legend says that the first Wilson who came down to south Florida won pretty much half of Florida in a poker game. Then brought his family down to start farming citrus and Florida's white gold, sugarcane. The Wilsons were beyond rich. Elite. Powerful. Everything I hated.

I didn't get too dressed up, after all, this was a high school party, but I needed to look the part and not stand out at all. I found some decent denim shorts, a white T-shirt, and nice leather flip flops that I bought from Sharon's Riches. Out of habit, I threw on a bathing suit first. You never know when you might need a swim. I told Dad I was going to a friend's house and wouldn't be home until late. I had no idea how long this would take.

It was dusk when I wheeled out of our driveway, and the sky drew darker as I rode closer to McCormick's. When I reached Blue Dolphin Lane, I could hear the music. Cars lined the street. Sweet. My plan is going to be perfect. The party had already started.

I slowed down. It was now pitch black. Like many times before, I nonchalantly whisked my bike into its hiding place. I was an expert at casing the mansion, having been here so many times. I decided to circle it once, looking for a possible easy access and making sure McCormick hadn't come to town. The place looked dark and quiet. Definitely vacant. I peeked at the party going on at Wyatt's and could see tons of kids around the pool in the back and dozens more just loitering around the mansion. I could easily blend in. Everything looked just as I had imagined.

It is now or never. My second circle around McCormick's showed no sign of easy entrance. I tried every door and window. Just as I was about to reach in my backpack for the heavy, jagged rock, out of nowhere popped Wyatt.

"What are you doing?" he asked with a smirk.

"Oh," I jumped and stammered and thinking quickly recovered with, "I decided to come to your party," I lied.

Wyatt looked around as if to question why I was, once again, in McCormick's yard instead of his, but said nothing.

Instead, he said, "Come here I want to show you something."

Chapter Sixteen

Not really having a choice, I followed him to a garage building that was separate from his mansion, where the party was raging. The music was so loud, I couldn't help but think how easily I could have busted a window without a soul hearing it. We walked silently through a side door into quiet darkness. He flipped a switch, and suddenly, I was in utter awe. I forgot all about the plate and that Wyatt had ruined my plan. This was no average garage. This was a science lab. A science lab and mechanic's paradise. Tables arranged in a maze-like pattern with neatly organized projects in the works. It looked like half of an airplane was in one corner and a muscle car without a hood in another. Like a fancy auto shop, a lift for raising cars had another unrecognizable sports car hanging in mid-air. The room was immaculate and filled with tools and all sorts of cool gadgets used for building things, I guess.

"This is my workspace," Wyatt showed me around, clearly impressed with himself, as he should be.

I forgot I hated him, momentarily, and blurted, "This is amazing." I kept looking around at everything in mind-blowing shock.

"I love science and building and fixing things, mainly electronics, cars, and my true passion-aeronautics," Wyatt said.

Slowly, I wandered around the vast workspace, looking closely at all the unique things. There was an exposed shelving system flanking an entire wall with precisely organized auto parts, computer parts, and a menagerie of mechanical devices. There was one whole wall with airplane propellers hung on display, some modern steel and others, wooden antiques. Next to the propellers, was a shelf filled with drones, drone parts and remote controls. There was a U-shaped desk area with four expensive-looking computers with large monitors. The space looked like a mini air traffic control center.

I was speechless. I stopped to stare at a collage wall with overlapping pictures of helicopters and airplanes, some in color and others in black and white. Aeronautics was definitely an obsessive hobby of Wyatt's.

"You like airplanes?" I asked the obvious.

"Yea, especially helicopters," he replied. "That is why I wanted to go to Lorenzo. They have the best A & P mechanics and Avionics program in the state."

He walked over to the collage wall and stood next to me. Pointing to a red helicopter, he said, "My dad's pilot taught me how to fly that."

Impressed, I said, "You know how to fly a helicopter?"

"Yes, and a Cessna and a seaplane. That red helicopter sits on our roof. The seaplane is out back. We keep the Cessna over at the airport." I immediately remembered the red helicopter descending the last day I came to steal from McCormick. Was that the day he saw me?

"My dad didn't want me to go to Lorenzo. He said he didn't want me going to school with poor delinquents that couldn't hack it at a *real* school. It pissed me off. I hated the bullshit I was learning in school. Everything was so useless," Wyatt gestured around the vast workspace. "I wanted to learn something I was interested in and when the principal from Lorenzo came to my middle school in eighth grade and talked about the programs they offered, I knew that is where I wanted to go. But my dad told me I had to go to Harvard, like he did, and study law. If I couldn't do something with aircraft, I would die," Wyatt continued, serious and shaking his head. "When he refused to let me apply in eighth grade, I went on a destructive streak. I got myself kicked out of every school in town until he would listen to me."

I wondered what exactly Wyatt did to get kicked out of so many schools in one year. Whatever it was, it must have been bad. And it worked. He is at Lorenzo, so I guess Wyatt was a spoiled rich kid who got what he wanted. He just wanted something I didn't expect.

Suddenly feeling awkward and unsure of what to say next, I blurted, "I better get going."

"But you just got here? I thought you came to the party?" Another smirk.

Ignoring him, because I had no good comeback, I headed for the door, and he followed behind me. Wyatt clicked the light off as we exited into the loud, muggy, dark night.

"Vivian?" I abruptly turned and felt my face flush. Leo was standing in the driveway next to the garage. "What are you doing here?" He sounded upset. My eyes adjusted to the darkness, and I could see his tall, tense body and mad face.

I turned to look at Wyatt, and he seemed equally interested in how I was going to answer this question. I couldn't say what I was really doing here, which was attempting to steal a $60,000 Picasso plate from a monster who beat my mother and wrecked my family. But I didn't want to tell Leo I was coming to Wyatt's party, either, because that was a lie—a lie that would hurt Leo unnecessarily.

I quickly recovered with, "I was going for a late-night swim and bumped into Wyatt." It was a lie, but I did have my swimsuit on under my clothes just in case. You never know when you will need to melt into the sea to escape.

This was a plausible lie because Leo knew my passion for swimming and that this passion sometimes led me to swim at weird times, however, Wyatt wasn't buying it. I could tell by his stare that he knew differently. After all, why would I be in McCormick's yard if I had come to the beach for a swim? In fact, I didn't need to go near Wyatt's or McCormick's houses to swim at the beach. Looking at Leo, I realized he was questioning the lie, too, probably wondering why I came in this direction if I was going for a swim. Wondering if I wanted to see Wyatt.

I wanted to flee this very minute. I wanted to run into the crashing waves and swim away. Swim away from lying, stealing, Dad's drinking, Mom's medical bills, Leo's judgement, and Wyatt's wealth. Swim away from the corrupt person I had become. Yes, that is what I wanted to do this very minute, so I blurted out, "Let's go."

"What?" Leo looked bewildered.

Wyatt's face lit.

"Let's go swim," I said and began walking towards the street.

I didn't look back. I knew they were both following me. Even if they weren't, I didn't care. All I cared about that minute was escaping into the Gulf.

Chapter Seventeen

"You are just going to leave your party?" Leo asked, clearly not wanting Wyatt tagging along on a night swim at the beach with me.

"They won't even know I'm gone," Wyatt wasn't turning around or slowing down.

I was walking fast. A beach swim consumed me. I needed to hide from my lies in the dark salty water. The minute we hit the sand, I threw off my flip-flops, t-shirt, and shorts. I had picked a skimpy bikini that wouldn't show through my clothes, and for a split second, I was self- conscious of how much skin was showing. But that quickly faded when I ran crashing into the surf. I popped up and turned around. Both Leo and Wyatt were just standing in the sand staring at me, fully clothed.

Realizing they weren't wearing swimsuits and didn't quite know how to join me in my sudden escapade, I taunted, "Come on. Scared?"

I was not prepared for Wyatt's bold move. First, he pulled his t-shirt over his head, exposing an unexpected muscular body. Then he stepped out of his shorts and dropped his underwear.

"What are you doing?" I screeched and laughed while waves pushed me around. I quickly turned, but not before glimpsing his naked body.

Not answering, he came diving into the water only a few feet from where I was.

I turned back around to see Leo taking off his shirt and jeans but leaving his boxers. He dove in swimming right towards me.

"Look, there's a full moon," Wyatt playfully dipped under the water exposing his buttocks. Both Leo and I laughed and began horsing around. Wyatt resurfaced and teased, "You know it is shark feeding time," and under he went again, yanking my leg from under the water, making me screech.

The waves were getting rougher, and we began body surfing. When Wyatt made it to shore, his naked backside shone brightly in the moonlight. He didn't seem to care. Leo loosened up and started joking around, "Hey, don't scrape the goods." I made sure to turn around whenever he started to stand up. After endless surfing, we finally tired of our night swim and Wyatt strutted without shame to retrieve his clothes, dressing in full view.

Leo and I slugged out of the water's wake and all three of us laughed and joked as we walked back to the party. My t-shirt stuck to my wet bathing suit and my hair dripped down my back.

"I'll get you guys towels," Wyatt said as he disappeared into the house. Leo and I waited while more and more kids showed up to party. The crowd was getting huge. No one commented on why we were wet, as if being soaking wet at Wyatt's party was normal. Leo was playfully hugging me, and I glanced over for a second at McCormick's mansion, where the plan I had made to steal the Picasso plate took an unexpected turn but ended up being pretty fun.

I suddenly stiffened up. There was a light on at McCormick's that wasn't on before. Then I heard a voice. A deep, older voice. I snapped away from Leo and turned towards the swimming pool. There on a lounge chair with two high school students sitting next to him was the slime ball McCormick. He stopped his conversation as if my glare was audible and looked right into my soul. A snake-like sneer formulated on the geezer's face as our eyes locked in contempt.

Leo followed my stare. The world started to spin. I wanted to run back to the beach. I wanted to crash back into the violent waves and swim and swim and swim. Swim away from here. Instead, I ran to my bike in the bushes without waiting for Wyatt or saying a word to Leo.

I peddled off, escaping into the night, like an exposed roach.

Chapter Eighteen

Headlights followed a few feet away as I raced home. I knew it was Leo in his car. I coasted into my driveway and Leo pulled up to the curve and quickly got out.

He ran towards me. "Viv, wait up." He gently grabbed my arm trying to pull me close for a hug, but I jerked away.

Displaced anger caused me to spew at Leo, "What were *you* doing at that party? You have some nerve acting like I betrayed you or something by being there, but what about *you*. What were *you* doing there? Spying on me? Were you following me? How dare you? I don't want you following me around. If I wanted to go to a party, I don't need your permission." I marched my bike into the garage, shutting the door firmly behind me, leaving Leo behind.

Chapter Nineteen

The house was silent, dark, and heavy. Heavy with trouble again. I could feel it. I could feel the stress pressing down on our cute little cottage with its window boxes of flowers, colorless gray in the dark hours of the night. Colorless. I could see their petals gently flickering right outside my window with the hint of moonlight casting a faint shadow.

I turned over and stared at nothing as I lay on my back on clean, cotton sheets. I didn't even bother changing out of my sticky clothes and damp bathing suit. I didn't have the energy. I was physically and mentally spent. Why did I act that way to Leo? Regret and remorse filled my mind. I wasn't mad at Leo. I was mad at McCormick. Why did those words spew out of my mouth?

But why *was* Leo at Wyatt's party? *Was* he following me? *Was* he worried I would cheat on him? Wait. We weren't dating. Did he think we were dating again? And what was McCormick doing at a high school party? You know the answer to that, Vivian. Preying on young girls. He nearly beat my mom and raped Bella and

Brianna, but there he was, audaciously lurking around a high school party. *He* is who I wanted to scream at, not Leo.

Exhaustion overtook my overcrowded, over-worried, over-angry mind.

***

There was complete darkness. No light from streets, buildings, stars, or moon. Deep, dangerous darkness. My body was bobbing up and down, floating effortlessly like a buoy bouncing freely, untethered. Sudden panic clenched my chest. Where was I? How did I get here? Why is it so dark? What am I doing bobbing in the sea? Something yanks at my leg. I jerk away and start to swim frantically. I don't know what direction I'm swimming—dangerously further out to sea or safely towards the sandy shore?

In the increasing darkness, a light appears, more brilliant against the black backdrop. The light comes closer and closer until it blinds me, and I turn away.

I sat up breathing deeply. Another nightmare. My mouth was dry and in desperate need of water. I got out of bed and stumbled through the dark house, making my way to the kitchen, where a small lamp sitting on the kitchen counter barely lit the space.

Dad was slunk at the table, head slung forward with his chin touching his chest, asleep, with a box of empty wine laying sideways next to an almost empty glass clutched in his hand.

Chapter Twenty

Fear almost overpowered my intense thirst, sending me fleeing back to my room, but my need for water rationalized my motions. I quietly got a glass out of the cupboard and turned on the sink, filling the glass and gulping the tepid liquid with primal need. I filled a second glass and drank it slower, still emptying its contents. Satisfied and now wide-awake, I glanced at the clock on the oven: 3:33am.

Thinking clearer now that my brain was rehydrated, I stared at dad, wondering what to do. First, I threw the box in the trash. Then I carefully extricated the glass out of his gentle grasp, leaving him sleeping. On my way back to my room, I cracked open the door to my parent's room and saw my mom sleeping peacefully.

I tiptoed back to my room and shut the door, locking it. Knowing sleep would be unsuccessful, I paced around my room cleaning and organizing, trying to busy my troubled mind. While reorganizing my closet, I pulled out the box at the very bottom of a neatly stacked pile of books. I slowly opened it. There was the Deepsea Rolex. Gorgeous. I took off the forty dollar watch I still wore from the Priceless Pawn and slipped on the magnificent piece of jewelry, clamping the clasp on the tightest setting. It was a man's watch, and the face was enormous on my slender wrist. I didn't care. It looked amazing. The blue-black dial illuminated against the stainless-steel band. Rolex was printed in green under the center where the hour, minute, and second hands met. Right under the word Rolex was the word 'Sea-Dweller' in smaller white print. Sea dweller. I was suddenly in love with this watch. The second hand had a tiny round diamond on it and ticked clockwise rhythmically. Hypnotized, I watched the tick, tick, tick.

I didn't want to sell it, but I needed to. Now. Before I fell too in love with it. I needed the money. I hated that I needed the money. But I had to pay off mom's medical bills. It will probably be enough. On Monday, I will take it to school and walk to the Priceless Pawn and have Roy list it for sale. Maybe I won't need to steal the Picasso plate. Maybe I will make enough to pay off our debt. I felt better. I took off the watch, put it in the box and began to breathe easier. I put it back on the bottom of my stack of books and noticed light coming in the window. Morning. Birds started chirping and the flowers regained color....... pink, blue, and yellow.

Chapter Twenty-one

I showered, dressed, and went to check on dad. He was gone already.

Maybe I'm overreacting about the wine. Maybe dad wasn't having a melt-down. He got up and went to work on his job sites, didn't he? That's a good sign. He wasn't passed out on the couch. I looked in the trash and saw the box of wine I threw away last night. I cinched up the bag and walked out to the garage to throw it away in the large trashcan. When I lifted the lid, I saw three more empty wine boxes.

Oh no. *Nooooo!* A knot tightened in my belly. I was fooling myself to think it was ok for an alcoholic to have just a couple glasses of wine. Foolish. How much longer before he goes back to the couch? How much longer before he gives up?

I have to help dad. Show him everything will be fine. Show him we can get through this, without wine. Show him there is a way out of the debt. I must sell that watch on Monday. I can't lose Dad again.

Chapter Twenty-two

I checked on Mom, and she slept as usual. In fact, she slept most of the time. I needed to occupy my mind so I wouldn't think about what a fool I was with Leo last night, or the fact that the scumbag McCormick is back in town, preying on girls a quarter his age. The thought of that man getting away with what he did, with what he was doing, nearly made my mind explode. I didn't want to go back to the beach, but I didn't want to stay here, where my mind was restless.

Sharon. That is who I needed. Sharon. She would be busy on a Saturday and need help. I also *needed* to see her. Sharon was strong. Sharon was peace. Sharon was my savior in times of trouble.

I changed into a pretty blue cotton sundress Sharon had picked out for me and slipped into strappy wedge sandals. I stepped out into blindingly bright light. I made it about a block before stopping to fumble around in my backpack for my shades. I didn't see what was creeping towards me until I looked back up.

There, right next to me, was a stretch limousine, with a window rolling down. I jumped, startled, too late to run away.

"Aren't you gorgeous. A younger image of your mother. I saw you at the party last night, but you ran off before I could get to know you. Didn't know you were a party girl. Why don't you hop in? I'll give you a lift to wherever you're going." McCormick. His voice was recognizably slimy.

He had some nerve showing up here. In my neighborhood. On my street. Was he stalking me? Stalking Mom? I was so creeped out. I wanted to run up to him and punch his face. Scratch his eyeballs out of their sockets. Instead, I picked up my pace towards Sharon's Riches, ignoring him completely while my heart beat wildly.

I faintly heard, "Uptight bitch like her mother."

Then I remembered Mom was home alone. Did he know where we lived? Of course, he did. A simple Google search can lead anyone anywhere. Why else was he on my street? I rounded the block and glanced at the limo continuing at a turtle's pace. Once I was out of sight, I cut through backyards, racing home to Mom.

When I got there, I slipped through my backyard, around the side of the house and looked up and down the street. McCormick's limo was gone. I raced inside to check on Mom. She was sound asleep. My heart was still beating rapidly. Why was that man coming near us? Was he stalking me? Was he stalking Mom? Should I tell dad? No. Dad couldn't handle it right now. I couldn't have dad any more stressed. Should I tell Leo's dad? No, if I got the police involved, Dad would have to get involved. I just had to be careful while McCormick was in town.

And I couldn't leave mom alone.

Chapter Twenty-three

I desperately wanted Dad to go to church on Sunday. I thought if he listened to the minister, it would keep him from touching the wine, but he said he had to work. The houses were almost complete. I thought of going myself but didn't want to leave Mom. I asked her if she thought she could go, but she shook her head no and gave me an 'I'm sorry' look with her eyes.

So instead, I did some homework, frequently glancing out the window looking for limos. I expected Leo to call me last night, but he didn't. Why would he? I'm the one who should be apologizing to him. What was stopping me? Pride? Not wanting to admit my behavior was wrong-again? I thought for sure he would call me on Sunday, and I was prepared to apologize. But he didn't.

When he hadn't texted or called by 10 p.m. Sunday night, I texted him. 'You picking me up tomorrow?'

No response.

Well, I would walk to school then. I didn't need Leo. Maybe I spewed those words at him for a reason.

What *was* he doing at that party? If he was checking up on me, I didn't like it. I didn't need to be checked up on. I can't imagine Leo going to that party because he just wanted to go to Wyatt's party. That was not Leo. The only explanation was that he wanted to see if I was there. I was the one who Wyatt invited. It had to be the reason he was there. And I didn't like it.

***

      The next morning, I was up super early. Today, I was going to get rid of the Rolex. I needed the money and with McCormick lurking around, I wanted it out of my house. I reached for the box and pulled it out from under the stack of books, opened the lid and took out the magnificent piece of jewelry. The Deepsea. Rolex. Sea-Dweller. I loved this watch. I didn't want to, but I did. I ran my fingers over the dark blue face and silver links. Strength. Power. Wealth. I didn't want to be materialistic. I wanted to hate it, but I couldn't. I loved how beautiful it looked. I loved how strong it felt, and I loved the name. Deep sea. Sea-Dweller. That was me. I am most comfortable in the sea. The expense of this watch represented the world I hated, and the name of this watch represented the world I loved, all in one fine piece of jewelry.

I slipped it on my wrist again and clamped it on the tightest notch. It was still a bit loose, but I didn't care. I felt powerful with it on, like I was violating McCormick. Taking something of his made me feel like I was stealing his power, and I wanted to feel that power all day. One last time. I was never going to step foot in his house again or go near that scumbag. I was never going to take from him again. He was getting too familiar. I didn't like it, and I didn't want anything to do with him anymore. I would sell this one last item, pay off my parents' bills, apologize to Leo, and everything would be OK. Forget the Picasso plate. I didn't need to steal it.

But today, I needed to feel that watch on my wrist, so I decided to wear it to school. Just one day I told myself. Then, at the end of the day, I would take it to Roy at the Priceless Pawn and sell it. I grabbed my Members Only windbreaker that I got from Sharon's Riches and zipped it up over my shirt. Even though the weather was far too hot for a jacket, it had sleeves that came down over the watch.

Just one day. What could it hurt?

Chapter Twenty-four

After I walked through the front door of Lorenzo, I headed straight for the Media Center to avoid seeing Leo. I thought back to when I escaped the roach scene in the cafeteria at Beachside Middle and met Leo for the first time. The Media Center was like that neutral country in a war, a haven for refugees. I sat at a round table and pulled out my assigned novel from English, *A Tale of Two Cities* by Dickens, and began to read.

The Media Center doors opened, and I looked up. My back stiffened instantly, and out of instinct, I lurched from my seat, grabbed my bag, and flew to a back study carrel to hide. I felt like a scared roach fleeing impending doom when a bright light flicks on. There, standing a few feet away, was McCormick with the Principal. I could hear them talking.

"This is our Media Center. Kids can study, use computers, and many take online classes here as well. Our students are on the fast track to graduate and begin their vocational training and many of them take extra classes online," Principal Rexford said, sounding like he was selling Lorenzo Williams Technical High School to this creep.

What the hell was McCormick doing here? Why would he be touring the school with the principal? Then Leo's dad's deep voice echoed in my brain, '*Misdemeanor violence charge. Community Service.*' Do not tell me this wretched human is doing his community service hours here. I wanted to shout to the principal to get that man out of here. The enemy was invading my safe place. I wanted to bolt but was cornered. If I got up now, they would see me.

"Well, thank you for the tour. You have an outstanding school here. Governor Wilson was right. Impressive programs. My foundation would love to support this school and that Shark Tank competition you mentioned. I was once a budding entrepreneur myself. Just tell me how much you need," the arrogant ass sounded so smug and full of himself. Typical, too. Instead of actually doing community service work, he was going to throw money around instead.

I was beside myself with fury. Did he know I went to school here? Was it a coincidence he chose this school to fulfill his community service hours? Or was he following me around town without me knowing? Was he taunting what he did to my mother in my face. But why? Maybe he was obsessed with me? He did lurk in my neighborhood and try to pick me up. What was wrong with him? He was sick. A sick, narcissistic predator.

Oh no. They stopped talking for a second. I felt eyes on me.

"Vivian, is that you?" Principal Rexford walked right up to the study booth. "I thought so! Vivian, this is Conrad McCormick. He is giving a sizable donation to our school today, and he has agreed to sponsor the Shark Tank competition. His rags-to- riches story is inspiring, and he loves to see students who are passionate about creating their own businesses."

Conrad's eyes lit with delight at having found me here. He had a giant grin on his ugly, old face. I could see his unexpected discovery was pleasing him immensely.

Suddenly, the walkie-talkie strapped to Mr. Rexford's hip blasted his name, and with a quick "Excuse me a minute," the principal left the room.

Alone with the man that I loathed more than anyone in the world, I began to excuse myself, too, and without thinking, stood up, snatching my backpack and book so quickly that my jacket sleeve slipped up and exposed my wrist.

McCormick's eyes narrowed, as I brushed the hair from my face, glimpsing the Deepsea out of the corner of my eye, and suddenly my heart stopped beating.

He grabbed my wrist hard. Too hard. I tried jerking it away but couldn't without causing a scene.

He sneered, "Look what we have here. A Rolex watch. What is a young girl from a poor school like Lorenzo doing with a Rolex watch?" With his other hand, he unclasped the watch, slipped it off my wrist, and shoved it in his pocket. "I think somebody has been snooping around my house," Our eyes locked in a hatred stare. "The next time you break into my home, I'll take something from you that you will never get back. Unless you have already given it away." He let go of my wrist but hooked his finger at the top of the zipper on my jacket and pulled me closer. I could feel his breath. "Are you a good girl or a whore like your mother?"

I wanted to spit in his face, but the door opened and quickly, Conrad McCormick let go and stepped back just in time for Mr. Rexford to rejoin us.

"Sorry about that," Mr. Rexford's kind smile was clueless to our heated exchange.

"That's Ok," McCormick said. "I'm leaving. Just call my secretary for a check." The two of them said goodbye to me, McCormick treating me like a casual acquaintance. Then they walked out the door.

And I was left standing in an empty library, without the Deepsea, without a way to pay off our bills, and in a shocking instance, without hope.

G. Keller

Chapter Twenty-five

Dazed from what had just happened, I walked silently to chemistry. I faintly heard Leo call my name in the distant crowd of kids making their way to class, but I didn't turn. I didn't have the energy. My plan ripped from my wrist in seconds. What a stupid decision to wear that watch. What was I thinking? Stupid. Stupid, stupid, stupid. Every time I seem to be getting closer to having everything normal in my life, a gust of wind blows me backwards.

Like a zombie, I managed to find my assigned seat. Wyatt was already at the table. "Hey," he said. "What happened to you Friday night? You disappeared and so did Leo. Are you two a thing?"

"No," I responded a bit too quickly. "I mean, we used to be, but we are just friends now." I wasn't even sure Leo would want to be my friend anymore, after yelling at him and ignoring him just now. I was pathetic. "I just needed to get home." Which is where I wanted to go right now.

Class started and the teacher announced a test Friday on the first unit. I let out a groan. I was going to fail this class. My GPA would plummet. I wouldn't get a scholarship. My mom's medical bills were going to make us lose our house. My dad was turning back into a drunk. I don't deserve Leo. I should pack up and go home.

"Come over and study with me. I love chemistry and can help you," Wyatt suggested hopefully.

"I can't." I didn't have it in me to elaborate. I didn't want Wyatt's help. I didn't want anyone's help. Right now, I wanted everyone to leave me alone. All I could think about was how that creep, McCormick, was ruining my life.

Thankfully, the teacher lectured through chemistry, saving me from any more conversation. At lunch, I chose to sit outside on a bench, and read *Tale of Two Cities*, ignoring the world. *It was the best of times, it was the worst of times, it was the age of wisdom, it was the age of foolishness, it was the epoch of belief, it was the epoch of incredulity, it was the season of light, it was the season of darkness, it was the spring of hope, it was the winter of despair, we had everything before us, we had nothing before us, we were all going to heaven, we were all going directly the other way—in short, the period was so far like the present period, that some of its noisiest authorities insisted on its being received, for good or for evil, in the superlative degree of comparison only.*

My English teacher said this was one of the best opening paragraphs in literary history. I read it over and over again, all through lunch, until I had it memorized. I think she is right. I loved it. I wonder why Dickens didn't say hell instead of 'going directly the other way.' Hell would have flowed better. Was hell such a bad word back then that writers couldn't use it?   Hell   was probably where I was going. Stealing. Lying. Hateful, murderous thoughts of what I would like to do to McCormick. I couldn't let that bastard get the best of me. I was slowly regaining my strength. I wasn't going to let him invade my space and taunt his power. He thought he was above everyone, above the law, with his billions of dollars. I was going to prove to him that money doesn't always win.

Roach Girl wasn't about to be stepped on by Conrad McCormick.

Chapter Twenty-six

I dreaded seeing Leo. Looking at Leo was like a giant reminder of how flawed I was as a human. His goodness just accentuated my 'going directly the other way' status. But we had class together after lunch, so I had to muster up the courage to confront him and apologize.

As I entered the room, he stood up and casually walked over to me and in true gallant fashion, gave me a warm, sincere, gentle hug. How did he manage to always be so kind to me, even when I didn't deserve it?

I started to speak, and Leo said, "Shhh, you don't need to say a thing." And I melted into him. I released the tension my body held. Why was I worried about what Leo would say? Leo loved me completely. He understood that McCormick was the one I wanted to yell at, not him. He understood my burst of anger. He understood I had been through a lot. He knew I had a complicated life. Had he not told me he loved me anyway? Hadn't he said he would be there for me if I let him?

"We need to start brainstorming ideas for the Shark Tank competition," Leo said and pulled away.

I glanced at Wyatt sitting alone in the corner of the room looking at us. I turned away and said, "I don't think I want to enter after all."

Chapter Twenty-seven

I walked home from school with all sorts of thoughts running through my head. What was going to happen to my family? How were we going to pay for Mom's medical bills? Could dad make enough money on future building projects to get us out of debt? Would he start drinking more and more and not even get future projects? Would Mom recover or require more medical attention? More medical bills?

These thoughts were weighing me down so much that I didn't hear the quiet motor creeping behind me……..until it was too late.

Chapter Twenty-eight

McCormick's window was down, and he was about to speak when I bolted. Like a light flicked on sends a hungry roach back to safety, I fled behind the first house in front of me. It wasn't ours, but I didn't care. I ran like an Olympic track star, hurdling flower gardens and kids' toys until I reached my backyard. I hid behind some bushes on the side of the house, waiting to see if the limo passed.

Chills trickled down my spine as I watched his limo creep by like a panther stalking its prey. My heart beat so loud and rapidly I could hear it. I stayed out of sight for a very long time, eventually sitting down to catch my breath. Just when I thought the coast was clear, I heard the hum of the limo again. I sat back down and watched as he crept by again. He was circling, like a shark. Fear paralyzed me as I realized McCormick was out to get me. Even though he should stay far away from my mother, the person he almost killed, he was stalking me. I should never have worn that watch today! I am so mad at myself. Now McCormick wants revenge. Should I tell Leo? Maybe he can convince his dad not to tell my parents. That is unlikely. He would have to tell my dad. This was serious. What if McCormick tries to hurt me? What if he tries to hurt Mom again?

I peeked around the corner of the house and looked up and down the street both ways. No limo. I ran into the garage and nearly stumbled over a bag next to the trash can. I looked down and could see through it. Opening it, I lifted an empty wine box. One, two, three, four. Four empty wine boxes. I was not telling anyone about McCormick. Dad couldn't handle the stress.

Chapter Twenty-nine

I sat on my bed and decided to study for the chemistry test on Friday, but every time a car passed, I jerked my head up to see who it was. I couldn't focus. How was I going to pass this test? The material was confusing and with everything that happened, studying was nearly impossible. I slammed the book closed and flopped back on my bed, staring at the ceiling.

Get it together, Viv. Don't let a scumbag like McCormick intimidate you. Don't let him scare you. Don't let him defeat you. You are Roach Girl. Remember? You lived on your own for six months without electricity, water, or money. You showered under a hose, you lived on peanut butter and resilience, you survived and thrived. Don't you dare let an old pervert who thinks money buys you anything and everything get under your skin.

I sat up feeling more confident.

The front door opened and closed. "I'm home." Dad.

I grabbed my chemistry book, shoved it in my backpack and shouted, "I'm going to a friend's house to study."

Chapter Thirty

My confidence grew with every pedal riding over to Wyatt's. I'm about to turn the tables on the old creep. He thinks he is stalking me? Ha! I am about to make his life a living hell. That's right, Dickens. I'm not afraid to say it. Hell. McCormick's life is about to become hell.

Chapter Thirty-one

Instinct told me Wyatt would be doing something in his garage workshop, and I was right. I walked directly in after one knock.

"Hey," Wyatt looked surprised but pleased.

"That chemistry tutor offer still open?"

Heaving my backpack on the table with a violent plop, I was determined to conquer chemistry and McCormick.

I was not going to let my dad become a drunk again. I was not going to let Mom's medical bills drown us. I was not going to let some worm of a human scare me. I might not have McCormick's Rolex watch to pawn, but I was going to take something better.

His Picasso plate.

Chapter Thirty-two

After two hours of studying, I was starting to understand chemistry. Wyatt was a genius.

"Come on. Let's take a break. I want to show you something." Wyatt stood up, and I followed him out the door and into the main house. The place was magnificent. A palace. Furnishings for a king.

"Where are we going?"

"I want to show you my favorite thing in the world." We climbed three flights of stairs and Wyatt opened a latch door on the ceiling of the third story. Yellow and red began to battle blue for dominance in the sky and a warm wind caught my hair. There in the middle of the flat roof was a shiny red helicopter. It was magnificent.

Like a kid, he excitedly led me to the aircraft's door and opened it, helping me climb in. Then he ran around and jumped into the pilot's seat. Once inside, Wyatt came to life, pointing out everything.

"Do you want to take it for a spin?"

"What? You can't fly this thing."

"Yes, I can. I have been training since I was a kid really. I started logging flight time at 14 and have been flying solo for six months."

I stared at him in disbelief. "Don't you need a parent or something?"

"Not anymore. You can fly solo at sixteen," he said. "Besides, no one is home. My parents are in Greece."

"Don't you need to tell a nanny or something?" I stammered, suddenly nervous, but exhilarated at the same time.

Wyatt scoffed and laughed, "What, do you think I'm five?" Wyatt's adventurous confidence sent a thrill through my body.

"You just stay in this mansion alone? No maid or anything?" I questioned, stalling as my mind ping-ponged the decision to do this or not.

"I'm home alone most of the time. The maids are here during the day, but they leave around four."

I was trying to calm my nerves. It was hard to imagine Wyatt flying this beautiful beast, alone. Excitement at doing something this radical electrified me, and after the day I had, I was ready to forget my problems for a while.

The sky was still light, and Wyatt said, "We will just go for a little spin along the shore."

Wyatt reached across my body, his arm touching against my chest as he grabbed the seatbelt, and strapped me in. Anxious energy coursed rapidly through my veins.

Within seconds, we were hovering above Wyatt's house and angling towards the Gulf. The large glass windshield wrapped around the aircraft, making me feel like a bird in flight, seeing everywhere and everything. As we swept over the water, I could see movement under the rippling waves. Then, in clear view, I saw gray shadowed outlines of sharks--tons of sharks—drifting slowly in smooth S-shaped motion. So many. Scattered like schoolchildren on a crowed playground, an ocean playground. A playground I swam in all the time. I had no idea this many sharks swam this close to shore. I must be surrounded by them when I go for my swims.

Further down the coast, I saw two dolphins gliding gracefully through the Gulf waters.

The sky grew darker and blue, yellow, and red turned to purple. Lights from the high –rise condos flickered and twinkled along the shore. I felt like a little kid in awe and wonder at the beautiful sights. Wyatt skillfully maneuvered the helicopter back towards his house, and I could see the green and white lights outlining the helipad. We eased gently down on the roof. I felt exhilarated. Powerful. Ready for anything.

I nearly bounced out of the helicopter and inhaled a slow, deep breath, wanting to remember everything, the smell of fresh, salty, sweet, machinery air, the night sky, the lights of Olde Portofino. The feeling was intoxicating.

"Want to swim?" Wyatt suggested next.

We were still standing on the rooftop looking out at the surrounding streets below. Reality began to push the past into the present. "It's getting late, and we have school tomorrow." I couldn't believe I had just uttered those words. Me turning down a swim was like a hungry shark passing by a juicy fish.

I looked at his face and it hit me. His eyes. His dark brown eyes held an emotion I understood. Wyatt's adventurous bravado could not hide the hint of haunting loneliness. He didn't want me to leave. He was alone. A lot. He was lonely. I remembered all the nights by myself when my parents disappeared. How incredibly lonely I was. Night after night with no one to talk to. Wyatt had to have friends he hung out with. Look at all the people at his party. But then I thought, he didn't really seem to talk to anyone at his party. He wasn't drinking. He hung out in his garage and left the party to swim with Leo and me. Suddenly, I didn't want to leave him alone.

"OK. I love to swim. But I don't have a suit," I said and before Wyatt could open his mouth, I laughingly shouted as we made our way back through the house, "And don't get any ideas about skinny dipping."

"You can borrow one of my mom's suits."

"That's OK. I'll swim in my shorts and t-shirt."

Wyatt's pool was Olympic size with a diving board at one end. Wyatt sprung high in the air and did a cannon ball, while I gracefully arced perfectly without a splash. I swam to the shallow end and Wyatt followed.

I was suddenly self-conscious swimming in the water with Wyatt. Why? We were just friends. Leo was the only guy I have ever had feelings for, so why was I suddenly uncomfortable?

We did a few handstand contests like little kids and playfully argued over who won. Then we dove off the board several times and finally I said, "I think I better get going," as I climbed out of the pool.

"We just started," Wyatt said.

I grabbed a towel Wyatt had retrieved from the pool house and began drying off the best I could.

"At least eat dinner with me," Wyatt urged.

I was sticky in wet clothes, but had a hard time saying no. "Ok," feeling less uncomfortable on dry land.

Inside, Wyatt opened a giant double- doored stainless refrigerator that was full of food. This was the opposite of my refrigerator when I lived alone.

"I'll make you my amazing super-smoothie. It is an all-in-one meal you will never forget," he boasted and began getting out pineapple, mango, yogurt, spinach, avocado, and then he reached for a banana in a huge bowl on the kitchen island. He opened a large cabinet for honey and spices.

Dumping everything into a space-age mixer, Wyatt blasted the high-speed machine until the contents were smoothly blended. He took out two large, expensive looking glasses and poured the lime-colored concoction evenly.

"Cheers," he said, and we clinked glasses. "Here's to chemistry, and helicopters, and night swims."

I smiled and echoed, "Cheers," took a sip and said, "This is amazing. What spices are in here?"

"My secret," Wyatt said.

We drank the smoothies and eventually sat on beautiful leather stools at the kitchen island.

"So, your parents travel a lot," I awkwardly made small talk.

"Yea, my parents have always traveled a lot. I think my mom thought it would be fun to have a kid, and my dad thought it would be good for campaigning. You know. Make it look like he was a family man. But my dad was born rich and so was my mom. They both love jetting all over the world. Without me. I am a hassle. Not as much fun as they thought. I had to go to school, doctor's appointments, you know, things that tie you down. I grew up with nannies and Legos and science kits," Wyatt said offhandedly. "I used to wish I was poor, with parents that couldn't go anywhere because they couldn't afford it. Parents that were forced to stay home and be with me," Wyatt kind of laughed it off as a joke, but I saw it was the truth. He continued, "But one thing I love about being rich is the helicopter. I have loved that helicopter since I was a little kid. My dad's pilot would take me for rides, and I was mesmerized. He taught me to fly at ten. By fourteen I had a learner's permit, but I was already a master pilot. The instructor who tested me told me he had never seen a young kid fly so well," Wyatt stopped. "Sorry, that sounds braggy."

It didn't really. Flying was his passion, and he didn't come across braggy at all. He came across as interesting and I said, "No it doesn't. You are passionate about something. That is cool. Not many kids are. You are lucky you found what you want to do with your life at such an early age. It is a gift." A gift born out of survival, I thought. Survival. My survival skills led me to remodeling homes.......*and* professional thievery, while Wyatt's survival led him to chemistry and helicopters.

I looked around the vast space. Wyatt was here in this mansion, alone as a little kid. Something I understood.

I looked at his face. Tan. Thick, wavy blonde hair. Chiseled cheekbones. His eyes were the opposite of Leo's—dark brown, almost black, like expensive Colombian expresso. I didn't want to like Wyatt. He represented everything I hated—wealth, power, privilege, entitlement. But I did like him. A lot. Leo had sensed I might, and that is why I saw glimpses of jealousy escape Leo's usual casual confidence.

When I met Wyatt, I thought I recognized him from somewhere. I couldn't put my finger on it. But I realized that what I recognized was something familiar emanating from his eyes. A look that I knew. A far-off look. Like he was often lost in thought. Yes, as I looked at Wyatt, I saw hints of myself. And not just that we both had thick blonde wavy hair, tanned skin, and brown eyes, but we shared an emotion. Loneliness.

We shared parent neglect, the scary feeling of being left alone far too young. Left alone for material pleasures, worldly vices. Left alone to cook for ourselves, entertain ourselves. We were both only children of rich parents, left because their parents loved money more than their children. No one knows how it feels to be 14 and left utterly alone—loveless—lonely—longing for rescue. Wyatt does. I recognized a look on his face. A familiar look. Lost. Living, but not really. Just existing—distant, depressed? Sort of—in a functional way. I saw this look on his face at school. I knew that look. People think you have it made when you have tons of money. Mistake. More money, more problems. No one gets it. But Wyatt does.

I don't know what compelled me to blurt out my story. Maybe it was that look in his eyes. A look I recognized. A powerful connection. Deep thoughts—dark thoughts. Dangerous thoughts. Wyatt was the opposite of Leo. Leo radiated goodness. He confidently understood right from wrong and like his father, held high moral standards that seemed to come effortlessly to him. Leo didn't have to work at being good. He was just good, naturally. Leo was a product of strong parental love, stability, devotion. Wyatt was mysterious, pensive, a paradox of good and bad. He held wild parties but didn't drink or smoke. He was brilliant but flunked out of every school in town. He was rich but dreamt of being poor.

Leo and Wyatt looked completely different, too. Leo was a modern-day mixture of cultures—caramel skin, blue eyes, controlled afro, lanky body. Wyatt had an ancient mixture of cultures reminiscent of early European settlers clashing with natives. His thick wild blonde hair and muscular body conjured up images of a Viking explorer wandering North America and falling in love with a Cherokee woman. His large almond eyes told a story of a lost soul searching for known peace.

Looking at Wyatt was like drinking truth serum, and once I started, I didn't stop. I told him how my parents left me on the same day, unknowingly, but still left me. I told him about how we lived in a mansion, but my dad turned into a drunk and lost his medical license. How my materialist mom couldn't take it and left—for Conrad McCormick. I told him about living in a gutted-out mansion with no food, water, air, and roaches for company. I told him about the cafeteria scene. Langston, Brianna, Bella, and Sarah and their betrayal. How I stole money to survive, and now, still have the urge to steal. How I give the money to the poor. About Conrad strangling and beating my mother to near death and getting away with it. The hate I felt for McCormick. How I can't stop stealing. How I hate money. How McCormick has been stalking me. How he came to school today.

I felt relief to share this with someone. I realized that as strong as I pumped myself up to be, I feared McCormick. His power and wealth were scary. I needed someone to know the creep was stalking me. Someone who wasn't afraid of wealth and power. Someone that wouldn't tell my dad or the police.

Wyatt watched me with concerned wonder. "Is that why you have been sneaking around his place all summer? I have watched you. I wasn't sure what was going on. McCormick always has girls at his place, young girls. He has always creeped me out. I thought maybe you were one of his groupies."

I shuddered, "God no. Gross."

"My dad is friends with the guy," Wyatt said. "And because of that, he has come over to a couple of my parties. I thought it was weird that the old dude was hanging with teenagers."

I had sudden remorse for sharing too much. "It is dark, and I need to get home." I stood up, grabbed my backpack, and put it on. "Thank you for everything. You really helped me with chemistry, and the helicopter ride was amazing. So was the smoothie."

"Let me put your bike in the trunk of my car and I'll drive you home," Of course Wyatt had a car and drives. Why wouldn't he? He had a helicopter and flies.

We walked out to the driveway to where I laid my bike down, and it was gone.

I looked around, suddenly panicked. "Where is my bike? I left it right here."

Wyatt and I walked up the driveway towards the street and looked all around. I went over to the bushes where I normally put my bike, and it wasn't there either. We walked back to the garage, looked inside, saw nothing, and walked back out. We canvassed the perimeter of the house, settling back where we started between the garage and the pool.

Someone took my bike.

A feeling swept over me. An icky feeling. I glanced over at McCormick's mansion. Lights were on.

Someone stole from me, someone who wanted to get back at me for taking his Deepsea Rolex, someone who has been stalking me, who wants me to be afraid of him, who threatened me if I ever stole from him again. A pervert who likes young girls. Conrad McCormick. It had to be him. Why did I leave my bike out in the open? Stupid. Just like wearing the Rolex. Stupid.

"The asshole took my bike," I blurted, enraged. "I want to go bust his door down and show him who is the better thief."

Wyatt stared at me, stone-faced, and instead of judging my irrational thought and telling me it is wrong to steal, he smirked and said, "Why bust his door down.... I have a key."

"What?" I uttered in bewildered disbelief.

"I told you my dad is friends with the guy. He came over like six months ago and gave my dad a key and the security code in case he needed my dad to go check on the place. My dad showed me the key and code because I'm the one who is always here."

I don't know what came over me. Maybe it was the fact that something was actually going to be easy for a change instead of so frickin' hard? Maybe it was the exciting helicopter ride or the night swim? Maybe it was the intimate conversation and realizing we had so much in common? Whatever it was, I sprinted to him and threw my arms around him and kissed him. It was meant to be an 'I'm so happy at this news, so I'm going to kiss my new friend to thank him' kind of kiss, but Wyatt reacted with instant passion.

He responded urgently, bringing his hands to my head, skillfully parting my mouth with his tongue, and instead of retreating, my body responded with equal urgency. My tongue mirrored his motion, and our bodies locked in sync. After a few hot seconds, I regained my sanity and pulled back, breathing heavily, staring at Wyatt in shocked confusion.

What are you doing, Vivian? Think about Leo. Leo is who you love.

Not Wyatt.

Chapter Thirty-three

Shocked at what just happened, we both stood paralyzed and silent.

"I, I, I'm sorry. I didn't mean to," I stammered looking at the ground.

Wyatt, relieving me of any further explanation, changed the subject and said, "So should I get the key?"

Oh yea, the key. The reason for my passionate outburst.

I thought for a moment and suddenly said, "No, that is what he wants me to do. It is bait. He wants me to come snooping. He is probably watching us now." Sudden goosebumps formed.

While my bike was my main mode of transportation, and I desperately wanted it back, all I could think about was one thing, the Picasso plate. The urge to take that plate consumed me. It was more than just needing the money now. It was the thrill of taking from that bastard. The thrill of a major heist. The thrill of stealing from McCormick gave me a jolt of power over him. I couldn't explain it. Did it make me a horrible person? Did my need to take from that rich scumbag make me a flawed human?

Yes. Yes, it did. But I couldn't stop. I couldn't rest until I had possession of the Picasso plate. But I needed to play it smart. No more stupid moves.

***

Wyatt drove me home in a blue Maserati. I thanked Wyatt awkwardly and crawled out of the car. I shut the door and turned around. Sitting on my front steps was Leo.

Chapter Thirty-four

I didn't hear Wyatt's car drive away. All I heard was my heart beating wildly. I knew this looked bad. Coming home late. Damp plastered hair from swimming. Clothes stuck to my body. Wyatt bringing me home in a sports car. What was I going to say to him? We were studying? We took a break to fly around town, swim, eat, share our souls, and make out?

It looked bad because it was bad.

And if I kept lying to Leo, I would never deserve him. Didn't we once say we would never lie to each other? Didn't I promise that? Haven't I already broken that promise and told myself I wouldn't do that again?

I put my head down and walked up to the house, rapidly deciding what to do. Is telling him half of what happened, and leaving the kissing part out, still lying? I didn't want to unnecessarily hurt Leo because the kiss was an accident. I didn't feel for Wyatt what I felt for Leo. Leo loved me when no one else did. When I was abandoned and lonely. When the world had turned against me for no reason. Leo was my rock. What happened with Wyatt would never happen again.

I forced myself to face Leo and looked up, catching a glimpse of the window boxes. The dark flowers perfectly still in the stagnant night air. The minute I looked into his eyes, I saw the sadness and worry and a silent thought bubble, *Is she slipping away from me again, this time for another guy? A rich guy? The ex-governor's son? The kind of guy she said she hated?* The hurt on his face was unbearable.

"It's not what you think," I uttered the worst cliché and immediately regretted it.

Eyebrow raised, Leo said, "Oh really, and what should I think?" As if that sentence clinched his already untrusting thoughts.

"I mean. We have a chemistry test on Friday, and I suck at chemistry and Wyatt is great at chemistry and he offered to tutor me," I rambled.

Leo looked me up and down, silently asking me about my damp clothes. Silently judging. Silently jealous.

Awkwardly replying, "We decided to cool off in the pool."

I was about to tell him about my stolen bike but stopped. I didn't need Leo telling his dad and getting the police involved. I wanted to handle McCormick myself, and Leo's dad would be furious if he knew I was anywhere near that man.

Then I started to get irritated even though I shouldn't have. I suddenly took the defense.

I had no right to get mad at wonderful Leo, but I blurted, "Why are you sitting on my doorstep?" I was sick of McCormick following me and didn't like Leo following me either.

"You wouldn't answer your texts, and I got worried. Your dad said you were studying with a friend, but I called Dushon and Dexter, and they hadn't talked to you either. I was worried," he repeated. Was he really worried, or was he using that as an excuse to spy on me? Leo looked less wonderful suddenly. Jealousy makes you ugly. Insecurity makes you vulnerable, less vibrant, weak.

"My phone died," I said, truthfully. I decided to do what I would normally do if I saw Leo. I walked up to him and slipped my arms around him. My irrational irritation with Leo vanished. He hesitated-which Leo never did when I hugged him-but regained his softness and hugged my back. I melted into him and thought, '*What would Leo do if he knew I had kissed Wyatt? How could I explain that away? Was it a lie not to tell him?*' I just couldn't tell him. I didn't want to hurt him. And what happened with Wyatt was a mistake. It was. It wouldn't happen again. It wouldn't. I silently repeated.

Chapter Thirty – five

I lay in bed, unable to sleep, even though I was utterly exhausted. What happened tonight with Wyatt? I went there to study and ended up flying in a helicopter, swimming, telling Wyatt dark secrets, kissing him? What was I thinking? What got into me?

Then I remembered the dream I had about the shark almost swallowing me up and the bright light from the helicopter saving me. Was McComick the shark? Was Wyatt rescuing me? But I am Roach Girl. I don't need rescuing. I rescue myself.

However, Wyatt *did* have the key to McCormick's mansion. The key that could make it easy for me to get back at McCormick. The key that could save my family from debt. The key that could save my dad from alcoholism and get revenge on the man that ruined my mother. McCormick had no right messing with my family. He had done enough. He needed to stay away from us, but for some sick reason he wasn't.

Why would that bastard invade my school today? Was it his community service requirement from the judge and just a coincidence? Was he really so interested in

Lorenzo's programs? Did he really want to give money to the school? Or was it just a ploy to get closer access to me? Did he find out I went to school there? It would be easy for McCormick to do. Just follow me one day. And hadn't he already proven he has been following me? The way he did today? McCormick should be in jail for what he did to my mom, for what he has done to young girls, and for who knows what other crimes he has committed.

Why would he go near *me?* Did he know I've been stealing from him all summer? Did he have cameras I could not see? I thought I looked everywhere for security cameras and didn't see any. Maybe he just wanted to stalk me because I looked like a younger version of my mom, and he likes young girls. McCormick was a predator. A predator stalking me.

A chill shivered through me. Get tough, Vivian. Get tough Roach Girl. You are not about to let an old, ugly, narcissistic man stalk you or violate you just because he is rich and thinks he is above the law. My mom may have been your victim, but not me. I am nobody's victim.

I survived when everyone left me.

I thrived when no one thought I would.

I am indestructible.

I am Roach Girl.

Roach Girl origin trilogy three

Chapter Thirty-six

By morning, I hatched a plan to begin messing with McCormick. He was messing with me by invading my school, following me home, and stealing my bike. I needed to take the offense. Turn the tables.

I was going to stalk *him.*

I was going to make *him* scared of *me.*

This shift in my mindset empowered me.

I am a survivor.

I walked out to the back corner of our yard to see if my little roach trap had any roaches in it. It did. I was going to start by taking back my bike and leaving my calling card.

Then I would move on to higher stakes. The Picasso Plate.

I am not going to let this wretched human control me.

Watch out McCormick. You are about to be infested.

Chapter Thirty-seven

On Tuesday morning, Leo picked me up for school, and we chatted as if nothing happened last night. When I got to chemistry, I acted as if I hadn't even gone to Wyatt's house yesterday and rode a helicopter, swam in the twilight, drank unbelievable smoothies, shared souls, and kissed. And Wyatt fell into cue, focusing on an assignment we were working on, not mentioning anything.

Until the bell rang, and he said, "Do you want to come study again tonight? Look for your bike?"

"Yes," I said, briefly thinking this was going to get complicated but didn't care. McCormick was my total focus.

"I can pick you up if you don't have a ride," Wyatt offered.

"No, I'll ride my mom's bike," I said, thinking I didn't want Leo to see Wyatt's Maserati coming down the street. Leo only lived a block away. It was very possible. *Why Vivian? If everything was innocent with Wyatt, why do you care if Leo sees Wyatt picking you up or not?*

G. Keller

Thirty-Eight

Mom was moving around more yet still had no voice. When I got home at 2:00pm, she was sitting at the kitchen table, drinking tea. She scribbled a note that read, "How was your day?"

"Good," I said. "My bike was stolen at a friend's house yesterday. Can I take yours to go study with him again? He is a chemistry whiz and apparently, I suck at chemistry and need all the help I can get. We have a test Friday," I was sort of telling her, masking my already set plans as a question.

She scribbled again, "Your bike was stolen? We need to call the police."

Oh no. I didn't want the police involved. At all. I quickly recovered. "Well, I think it was a prank by some kids, actually. My friend is asking the neighbors about it. I think I'll get it back today. If I don't, we can call the police."

Mom looked skeptical. She wrote, "If you don't find it today, I am telling your dad, and we will call Leo's dad."

Oh, I'm getting it back today.

G. Keller

Thirty-nine

"Let's go for a helicopter ride," I blurted as I wheeled into Wyatt's driveway and saw him walking towards his garage.

He didn't hesitate or ask me why. He just said, "Let's lock up your mom's bike."

We ran with giddy excitement up to the helicopter pad, and within minutes, we were scaling the shores of Portofino like majestic predatory birds.

Again, I marveled at what I could see from the sky. Fish schooling below had me mesmerized. I was becoming addicted to this vantage point. Swimming will always be my first love, but I was rapidly falling for flying.

"Look!" I shouted. "My bike!" I screamed, pointing at McCormick's mansion below.

Wyatt curved around for another fly-by, and there, next to his pool, was my bike.

He was baiting me to come get it.

"Let's go check it out," Wyatt yelled while positioning to land on his roof. The adrenaline rush from flying and anticipating my next move on McCormick had my brain working overtime.

Once out of the helicopter, Wyatt and I made our way back downstairs, hashing out ideas on how to get the bike back.

"We will just walk over there and take it," Wyatt insisted. "He won't harm you with me there. I am Governor Wilson's son." Wyatt's tone was playful, trying to lighten my mood.

"I don't want you involved," I said, thinking I didn't want Wyatt connected in any way.

"Why not? He took your bike. That is weird, and we *should* call the police on him."

"That will only make it worse. McCormick has connections higher than the police. He got away with almost killing my mom and drugging Bella and Brianna. Who knows what he has done to other girls. Taking my bike is child's play to him. He will just say it was in his yard or something. Then he will be out to get me even more. No. I am going to get it myself." I said adamantly.

I wanted to ask Wyatt for the key and security code, but knew I needed to wait for that. I wasn't getting the Picasso Plate today. I just wanted to get my bike. Show McCormick I wasn't going to submit to him. I wasn't afraid of him.

I continued, "Let's just go nose around a bit. Spy on him. I know a few places to hide in the bushes. Maybe I can swiftly get the bike without McCormick knowing."

Grabbing my backpack off the kitchen island, I slipped it on in case an opportunity to get the Picasso Plate arose. I missed the first chance to get it, and I didn't want that to happen again. Wyatt looked at me quizzically, but just smirked and said nothing, like he knew what the backpack meant.

We found a space I had hidden before and crouched down. I could hear Wyatt's nearly silent breathing, and his knee touched mine for a moment. I glanced at his profile, high chiseled cheekbones, full lips and thick, unbrushed curls of blonde hair gave me a rush of blood throughout my body.

Refocusing my energy to McCormick's yard, I uttered quietly, "Look, there is my bike." Suddenly the back sliding doors opened, and McCormick sauntered out to the pool deck with a drink in his hand. He stopped and gazed out at his backyard and yacht.

Wyatt whispered, "I have an idea. Follow me."

He grabbed my hand as we exited the bushes and began racing back to Wyatt's garage for safety. "I will knock on his front door and strike up a conversation with him. I'll invite him to my party Friday, tell him some girls want to meet him, puff up his ego, and you get the bike. Just lean it against the back gate and when I'm done talking to him, I'll meet you there and help you get it over. Can you jump the gate?"

He had no idea. "Yes, I can jump the gate."

I went back to our hiding place alone, while Wyatt walked casually to McCormick's front door. McCormick still stood out by the pool. Then I heard a loud chime, and McCormick turned and began walking into the house. I didn't hesitate. Like Spiderman, I scaled the rod-ironed gate that led to his backyard. I slipped around the mansion in a blink and saw the bike leaning against the wall. Then I noticed the sliding door slightly ajar.

Impulsively, I slipped inside McCormick's mansion and tiptoed swiftly to Conrad's bedroom, my heart beating wildly. I unzipped my backpack, pulling out the jar full of roaches. I glanced over my shoulder to the door and still heard faint talking and laughter. I pulled down the white comforter and sheets and unscrewed the lid, releasing hundreds of nasty, caramel insects into the bed. Unafraid of the grotesque critters, I reached my hand into the jar and helped the remaining bugs find freedom.

I shoved the jar back in my backpack, glanced down the hallway toward the office and was about to dash down there to grab the plate, but Wyatt's voice got louder. Taking the cue, I slunk out of the house in lightning speed, grabbed my bike and hustled it to the hedge-flanked rod-iron fencing that separated McCormick's yard from Wyatt's. With strength earned from years of swimming and biking around town, I hurled my bike over the fence myself. I didn't need Wyatt's help. Then I hurdled myself over, barely brushing the bushes beneath my body.

I picked up the bike and wheeled it into Wyatt's garage, peeking my head out the side garage door, waiting for Wyatt's return.

When I saw him, I whispered loudly, "Over here," and waved him into the garage.

Stunned, he saw the bike and said with an impressed smirk, "I guess you didn't need me to help you get it over the fence."

"I guess not," I smiled back, heart still racing.

Without hesitation, he walked directly to me, grabbed my head with his hands like he had done yesterday, and kissed me with determination and desire. My body, still reeling from the adrenaline high of what I had just done, responded with passion I couldn't contain. We couldn't stop. My hands found their way around his waist and circled his back. Taking my aggressive cue, Wyatt moved his hands over my shirt, grazing my breast slowly. Sensations flooded my body, and I realized I hadn't felt this euphoric feeling since Leo and I made out on the beach by the Pointe Palace. Leo. The thought stopped me cold. I can't do this. I love Leo.

"Stop," I whispered reluctantly. Wyatt sensed I didn't really want to stop and kept kissing me. My lips kept kissing him back, sending confusing signals. I managed to pull away and more forcefully say, "No, I mean it. Stop."

Wyatt stopped. I looked at the ground. I couldn't look at him. I didn't trust myself. "Can you take me home? Put both bikes in your car?"

"What about studying chemistry?" Wyatt sounded disappointed.

"I think I better get out of here with the bikes. I am sure McCormick has noticed my bike is gone," I said.

"All the more reason to stay until it is dark. Wait until he loses your scent."

"What if he goes trolling my house? My mom is there."

"Call your dad and tell him you will be late. That I'll bring you home. Tell him to go check on your mom. Maybe he is home."

I thought for a minute. This all sounds logical. And I did need to study chemistry, badly. I hesitated and then decided to call dad. He was home. Mom was fine. I told him I would be home around 9 p.m. When I hung up, I stared at Wyatt, and he stared at me with intensity and longing.

He took a step closer to me and suddenly there was a pounding at the garage door and a jiggling of the locked handle.

Chapter Forty

I jumped and Wyatt jerked his head around. Wyatt gestured for me to hide. I swept my bike and mom's bike quickly behind a back wall and crouched down in a hidden corner, my heart beating loudly.

"Wyatt! Vivian!"

Leo.

Thinking fast on my feet, I popped up and ran to the door, opening it rapidly, and pulling Leo into the garage and out of view. Shutting the door and locking it behind me, I hugged him quickly and said, "It's you." My quick thinking disarmed Leo from wondering what might be going on between Wyatt and me. "McCormick stole my bike yesterday. I didn't want to tell you because I knew you would get your dad involved, and I didn't want to go to the police. Wyatt helped me steal it back." I pointed to the bike in the hidden corner.

Leo looked bewildered at the news.

"What are you doing here?" I asked, surprised to see him.

I texted you and you never answered. I called your dad, and he said you were studying with a friend. I figured you were studying chemistry with Wyatt. Since I was working down the street, I thought I would stop by."

Leo suddenly looked embarrassed. His pounding on the door a minute ago had the sound of anger and urgency, not a 'hello, thought I'd stop by'. I didn't like this jealous Leo. But I didn't like myself for sneaking around on him, causing his angst. I felt caught, but worse, I felt responsible for his insecurity.

They stood side by side, Leo and Wyatt, looking at me. Leo, a head taller than Wyatt, with his smooth caramel skin and aqua eyes the color of the sea, was gentle, quiet. Wyatt, with his blonde, unbrushed locks, tan, muscular body, and dark intense eyes, was bold, brave. They radiated an image of polar opposites. As they stood and stared at me, I realized something. I liked them both. I didn't want to like Wyatt. He was privileged, entitled, and spoiled. Who has their own Maserati and helicopter? This garage/mechanical science lab was equipped with every expensive gadget imaginable. Wyatt represented everything I hated—uber wealth and luxury beyond what is necessary. Why did I like him? How was it possible to like two such different people? I thought I would only love Leo and that when you fell in love, that was it. But my feelings were confused. When I was with Leo, I felt peace and comfort.

When I was with Wyatt, I felt adventurous and spontaneous. Could I be in love with two people....at once?

I snapped out of my troubled mind and suddenly wanted to flee. "Excuse me," I said and escaped to the bathroom in the back corner of the garage. Once inside, I looked at myself in the mirror. Why do they like me? My brown eyes stared back at me in wonder. As I stared intensely into my eyes, I noticed something. The color. Brown, but not dark espresso brown like Wyatt's. They were a kaleidoscope of copper and various shades of amber, like the colors of a roach. Roach Girl. Why would they like Roach Girl? I was a thief, a sneak, and full of bitterness and anger. Bitter over what my life had turned into over the last few years. Angry at dad, mom, money, and McCormick.

I constantly wondered why bad things happened to me. Why couldn't I have a normal family? Why did my dad drink? Why did my mom need clothes, shoes, and a fancy house? Why was money more important than me? Why did she leave me for a creep like McCormick? Why did I need to steal? Why did it bring me so much satisfaction? I didn't want to feel this way. People say I'm pretty. Is that the only reason they liked me? Were boys that shallow? As I looked at my long, wild blonde hair and roach-brown eyes, I didn't feel attractive at all.

I felt ugly. I didn't deserve either one of their affections. I wanted to go home. I didn't want a boyfriend. I would only bring them trouble and pain, like the pain I was causing Leo.

I exited the bathroom and grabbed my bike. "Leo, can I put the bikes in your car, and can you take me home?"

"Sure," he seemed all too eager, rushing back to grab my mom's bike. Wyatt helped load the bikes, and I said I would see him tomorrow.

As we pulled out of the driveway in silence, I looked over at McCormick's mansion. Conrad was standing on his massive front steps, arms folded. Our eyes locked, and I refused to look away. Conrad didn't flinch and neither did I, as the hatred passed between us.

Chapter Forty-One

Exhaustion swept over me like a tsunami, sending me to bed immediately after dad insisted I eat something. I briefly noticed the clock on my nightstand glowing 8:02 p.m. as my eyelids closed and wondering if I had ever gone to bed this early. With so much stress the past two days, along with a sleepless last night, my body easily pulled me into the depths of deep sleep and deep dreams.

In the silent car ride home with Leo, I decided I didn't need or want a boyfriend in my life. I wanted to avenge my mother's honor against the scumbag McCormick and get my dad back on track with no bills looming over him, causing him to slide into a wine glass. I didn't need distractions from a love triangle. But drifting off to sleep in my dark bedroom with only the glow of the clock, I found myself imagining the summer I first met Leo, imagining swimming in the blue Gulf waters, imagining our bodies locking together, imagining discovering each other for the first time.

Then the kissing grew more passionate, and I ran my hands over Leo's back and chest. The salt from the sea and the heat from the sun fueled our desire. I needed love, the love I was lacking from the desertion of my family. Leo responded to my advances with equal urgency. He cupped my head with his hands, kissing me deeply. My hands found his head, and I realized in my euphoric moment that I had grabbed blonde locks not black ones, and I pulled back to see it was Wyatt now and not Leo. Confused, I staggered away into darkness and tripped backwards falling, falling, falling into an abyss...... then floating, floating, floating like an astronaut without a spaceship....... Suddenly, I was bobbing, bobbing, bobbing in dark waters. Total blackness. No stars to offer light. I felt a ripple under the surface. I looked and a shark's fin cut free and began circling me slowly. Then it disappeared. Out of nowhere, a blinding spotlight broke through the invisible clouds, descending slowly upon me. A rapid propeller fanned my face and rippled the waters. I felt a nip at my feet from the depths of the sea and jolted in sheer terror......a stretcher dropped from the red helicopter, and I grabbed it, hoisting myself onto the makeshift bed and strapping in....the helicopter took flight without lifting me into the cabin....I was dangling midair, swinging back and forth in the sky as the helicopter took me on a joy ride skirting the coast.....lights from the high-rise condos twinkled like diamonds....Then, I felt a tickle and a roach crawled out from the sheet on the stretcher....then another and another until roaches were crawling all over me. I couldn't move. I was strapped in and sailing through the sky. Roaches crawled on my face and in my hair. I tried to free my arms to get them off me, but I was trapped and couldn't move. I squeezed my eyes and mouth shut keeping the roaches from entering my body. No use. There were swarms. They tunneled into my ears and nostrils. I couldn't breathe. I couldn't breathe. Help! Help!

I woke with a small cry, panting and gasping and sweating. I frantically looked around. Where was I? My room. I was in my room. I was dreaming. The house was silent. My room was black. Then, I jumped again. I felt a tickle on the back of my neck and reached to find a roach, a leftover from leaving my calling card at McCormick's no doubt. He must have hitched a ride on me.

Suddenly, I heard a noise, and a bright light shone through the blinds of my window. Someone had pulled into our driveway. I glanced at the clock, thinking it was three or four in the morning, but it was only 11:30 p.m. I had gone to sleep so early, it felt like I had been out for hours.

Curious and scared, I carefully pulled back the blinds slightly to see who was there. A limo had awkwardly tried to pull into our little driveway. Only the front end of the car could fit, while the rest jutted diagonally into the street. Its headlights pierced my room with blinding brightness. My heart went wild with worry. What was McCormick going to do? Had he come to get me? Kidnap me? I froze while peering out the side crack of my blinds. After moments in my driveway, the limo pulled away. I watched as the taillights drifted down the block and out of sight.

I waited......... I watched....... I worried..........

Suddenly, headlights lit the street, growing brighter as the car grew closer. I shuddered as McCormick's limo crept by again. This time not bothering to turn into the driveway, just slowly driving by.

After the taillights disappeared again, I waited....... I watched....... I worried.........

Trying to breathe normally was nearly impossible. I could see my chest heaving up and down in the dark. Then, again, the lights grew in brightness and McCormick's limo drifted by my house a third time. He was circling me.

Like a shark.

McCormick was trying to tell me who is boss. Well, scumbag, if you think driving to my house late at night and shining your lights in my window will scare me away, think again.

I took a deep breath as the room grew dark once more. I will NOT be intimidated by you, Conrad McCormick. The darkness gave me confidence. The darkness emboldened me.

After a half hour went by with no limo drive-by, I laid back down, trying futilely to go back to sleep. I thought about my dream....my nightmare. I have had a similar version of this dream before. The helicopter, the sea, the shark. If I can get my family back in order and rid McCormick from my life somehow, I can find peace. No more nightmares. I needed that Picasso plate. Then I won't steal ever again. Any money I want for charity will come from dad's building business, RG Construction, and Sharon's Riches and any money I make in the future, not from stealing. I promise.

Once more and that was it.

I had to get my hands on that key and code, so I could slip in easily. McCormick was looking for me to snoop around his house. I had to go in when he was either gone or asleep. I didn't want Wyatt to have anything to do with this. I would need to somehow borrow the key from Wyatt and then return it without him knowing.

Chapter Forty-Two

It was only the second Wednesday of school, and it felt like we had been here for months. I understood chemistry a little more and when Wyatt offered to continue tutoring me, I hesitated a yes response. I didn't want to be alone with him. I didn't trust myself. Helicopter rides, late swims, long talks. Sexual attraction. I couldn't deny it. It had happened twice when I was with him. But I needed that key to McCormick's, so I said yes. I would just have to exercise more control.

At lunch, I asked Wyatt to join our table and could tell Leo didn't like it. I didn't care. Having both Wyatt and Leo at the table together was going to make it easier for me to begin treating them both as friends. Dushon and Dexter helped accomplish the 'friend' vibe.

After lunch, Leo, Wyatt, and I walked together into Entrepreneur class and all three of us froze as soon as we entered. There was McCormick—AGAIN. What was going on? I wanted to run away. I wanted to shout, *'What the hell are you doing here?'* But sudden strength engulfed me. I squared my shoulders and marched confidently—with my head held high—to my seat. Leo followed and Wyatt dutifully shook hands with his neighbor, saying hello and then sat.

Leo touched my arm and began to whisper, "Are you ok-"

"Shhh," I snipped. "I'm fine." Leo knew everything about McCormick and my mom and so did Wyatt after Monday's truth and make-out session. You could feel the tension at our table.

"Class, please be seated quickly. We have a special guest," Mr. Miller said, smiling. When the last kid was seated, Mr. Miller continued, "I want to introduce you to Mr. McCormick. He is a self-made businessman and is here today to tell you about his rise to business stardom, give you some entrepreneurial tips, and tell you about the Shark Tank competition his corporation is now sponsoring. Mr. Rexford told him all about it and after a very impressed visit on Monday, he wants to fund the school and county contests."

I sat there livid, wanting to lurch from my seat and strangle him in front of everyone. I hated the audacity of this man. I hated how money and power could snow everyone into thinking you are an upstanding citizen. When really, all you are is a rich thug. A rich thug flaunting his power. A corporate bully who thinks a little 15 -year-old girl is no match for his worldly rank.

I have news for you.

I am the girl who is going to infest your glitzy life with a swarm of trouble that you are not prepared to handle. I am younger, faster, stronger, and angrier than you. My hatred of you is going to fuel a plan so clever, you will never outwit me. You think coming to my school and throwing money around here will get you access to me? To other young girls? Think again. You are just a rich pedophile, and I am about to bring you down, old man. You hurt my mom, and as a result, hurt my dad, and now you invade my school? You just made my revenge so personal. You are going to wish you were dead when I am through with you.

My eyes must have been spewing hate because he looked right at me and sneered. I could tell he liked what was evolving between us. He was sickly turned on by our feud. His eyes screamed 'bring it on pretty girl. This is just what I want. A young girl going after me.'

I am not a pretty girl, geezer. I am Roach Girl. Ugly, nasty, mean, and indestructible. I am going to crawl inside your mansion and rip you off and leave my mark. And you will not catch me. Never. If you think you can win against a roach, think again. I will just keep popping up and popping up until you have nothing left.

I listened to McCormick drone on like the most narcissistic human on the planet, boasting of his businesses and billions. I tuned him out before throwing up and started a mind fantasy of ideas on how I was going to get the Picasso plate from him. But what then, Vivian? Say I get the plate from him and managed to sell it online without him knowing. That won't stop him from harassing me. It will only make it worse. Will he even know the plate is gone? I could put a fake in its place, and he may not notice. I liked that idea. It would buy me time at least. It may take him months or years before he would recognize it was a fake. By then the plate would be sold, our bills paid, and my dad sober again. But how could I stop the harassment? He is proving he won't leave me alone. I could go to the police then. All of my money problems would be solved, and I could go to the police to get him to stop.

Vivian, you are crazy. He is not going to stop. Going to the police won't help. They didn't help mom when she was brutally beaten. Leo's dad tried, but McCormick's connections were too high up.

I was suddenly overwhelmed. Everything seemed too risky to pull off. Air was escaping my pumped-up self from only minutes ago. I can't do this. I can't defeat someone like McCormick. He is too connected. Too powerful. Too ruthless. It *is* true that money can buy you anything. Free reign over the poor. Look at how Mr. Miller is so impressed by him. Look at

McCormick's expensive clothes and shoes, all just a costume to cover his crimes.

Just as I was about to give up on the whole idea of getting back at McCormick, two things happened at exactly the same time. I saw the Deepsea watch on his wrist, baiting me, making me snap out of my defeating thoughts and second, he boldly said, "And I couldn't have been successful without amazing employees like Vivian's mother, Victoria." All eyes turned to me, and I felt myself flush. McCormick continued, "Vivian's mother was one of my best saleswomen and what a beauty. She could sell a fur coat to an animal activist. How is your mother? Send her my best and tell her she is always welcome to come back and work for me." His eyes lit with fire, as if toying with my emotions was a fun sport to him. His face glowed with the delight of thinking he got me, he one-upped me, he took the wheel, and I am a mere passenger on his ride.

The audacity. The narcissism. The gall of this beast to stand there in front of everyone and even mention my mom's name, to stand there and say what a great employee she was, to stand there and *invite her back to work for you?* What kind of delusional demon are you?

McCormick, you are a fool. I was about to cave to your power and quit my quest for revenge. I suffered a slight weak moment, a futile stomp, but I have sprung

G. Keller

back. You think wearing that watch frightens me? You think talking about my mom scares me? You think coming to my school intimidates me? Think again. I *was* shriveling. But now? Bring it on old man.

Bring.

It.

On.

The bell rang and students passed McCormick, shaking his hand, and thanking him for sponsoring the Shark Tank competition and coming today. A couple of girls I barely knew flirted with him, and I wanted to vomit. McCormick and Mr. Miller were talking as I grabbed my backpack to leave.

Then Mr. Miller turned to me and said, "Vivian, I need to speak to you."

Uh oh. "Yes, Mr. Miller?" I ignored McCormick.

"Mr. McCormick was just telling me that because he is funding this event," Mr. Miller stammered and looked down, reluctant to say what he needed to say. "Well, because he is funding the Shark tank event, you cannot enter. Your mom was once an employee of his and that is against the rules. I'm sorry, Vivian. I know you wanted that scholarship money, but there will be other scholarships."

I looked over at McCormick in slow motion. That bastard. His sinister grin dripped of satisfaction. Not only was I going to take the Picasso plate from you, you monster, I may never stop taking from you. I was going to stop stealing after the plate, but now? I will take and take and take from you until you are penniless. I will not be satisfied until I see you broke and in jail.

***

Leo and Wyatt were waiting for me in the hall. Leo said, "What was that about?"

"I can't enter the Shark Tank competition. Apparently, because my mom worked for him and he is sponsoring it, I can't enter. No scholarship chance for me."

"What an ass," Wyatt said.

Leo asked, "Are you OK?"

I stood there, stunned. How can a person be so cruel? Why? Why does he want to continue to hurt my family? What did we do to him?

"I'm fine," I lied. "With McCormick involved in the competition, I don't want to enter anyway."

Wyatt suddenly said, "Can you guys come to my house tonight? I have an idea."

Chapter Forty-three

I rode my bike straight into Wyatt's garage with such speed I doubt anyone saw me. Leo showed up minutes later, coming right after work from the home down the street.

"I know how you can get your scholarship," Wyatt paused, then said, "Leo and I will enter. We will all work on it together, here, after school, but only Leo and I will enter. If we win, I will donate my scholarship to you. We will outwit McCormick's attempt to steal your chance at the scholarship."

I stood looking at them again, side by side, like yesterday only different. United, not divided. My preoccupation with McCormick and revenge had squelched any desire to have a boyfriend, yet I could see they both had feelings for me. It wasn't as if they had Hallmark card puppy dog eyes or anything. It was their desire to do things for me. The way they were quick to be there when I needed them. Leo no longer had an insecure, worried he was going to lose me look, and Wyatt's eyes weren't lusting. They both just looked ready to slay a dragon for me.

I was about to tell Wyatt I didn't think they would let him just 'gift' me the scholarship money, and I could slay my own dragon and didn't need their help. Nor was the potential scholarship money at the forefront of my mind, but suddenly an idea popped into my head and immediately blew up like a helium balloon. If Wyatt, Leo, and I worked together on a project for the competition, we could meet here daily, increasing my ability to case McCormick, increasing my chance of getting the key to McCormick's mansion, and decreasing the love triangle problem by all becoming friends. While both Leo and Wyatt knew I had stolen from the rich in the past, they didn't know of my future plans to take the Picasso plate. They didn't know about my mom's medical bills and my dad's relapse into the wine box. Being here with them, working on a project, could be the perfect cover-up. No, the desire for scholarship money wasn't motivating me, but my home problems and McCormick's quest to continue to mess with me was.

Most of all, looking at both of them, standing there so gallantly, I realized Leo needed this scholarship and Wyatt needed the companionship. Leo was a senior and didn't have a scholarship yet. He had applied for several and hadn't heard. I knew his parents couldn't afford to send him to college. I knew that wouldn't stop him. He would work two or three jobs if he needed to in

order to go, but a scholarship would make things easier.
And Wyatt's parents were never home, leaving him here
in the lonely mansion night after night. It was neglect. I
understood the pain of that kind of loneliness. Yes, we
all needed each other. And with Wyatt's genius mind
and resources and Leo's work ethic and public speaking
talents, they had a good shot at getting the scholarship,
and I had a good shot at getting the revenge I craved, and
the freedom I needed.

Chapter Forty-four

When I got home, Mom and Dad were sitting at the kitchen table looking grim.

"Is everything ok?" I asked.

"The doctor said your mom's voice box was permanently damaged," Dad looked sad. "She will most likely never be able to speak normally again. The doctors think maybe, with a lot of speech therapy, she can gain some of her voice." That meant a lot of doctor visits and money.

Mom scribbled a note and handed it to me. 'It will be OK. I am fine." She smiled as I read it. She scribbled something else. 'I am feeling better. I would like to spend Saturday with you.'

Mom was reaching out, trying to mend fences. "Ok," I said, hesitantly. And I smiled a small, empathetic smile and left the room.

I didn't know how to feel about spending the day with mom. I had so many mixed emotions. Part of me felt sorry for her, permanently injured by McCormick, by bad decisions.

But part of me was furious with her, for leaving us, for leaving me, alone, because she couldn't handle a bad situation, because she wanted an easy way out. But if I wanted our family put back together, and I did, desperately, I had to try, too. Spending time together, as awkward as it will be, is the only way to move forward.

Chapter Forty-five

I told Wyatt and Leo that I couldn't meet after school because my mom needed me, but I agreed to meet them Friday night.

Wyatt said, "I tried to cancel Friday's party, but apparently, I can't stop the runaway party train. I'm going to put a big sign out front that this is the last party. It's getting old."

I was glad the party was still on. I needed Friday's commotion. I needed the loud, chaotic distraction to steal the plate. I needed McCormick to flirt with girls, so I could invade.

Chapter Forty-Six

On Friday, I showed up at Wyatt's before Leo. I wheeled my bike into the garage and leaned it against the wall. Wyatt had ordered pizza and soda and was tinkering with a drone.

"Hey," I said casually.

"Hey. Come here. I want to show you something," Wyatt got up and walked over to a red and silver metal cabinet, opening the top drawer. "This is the key and code to McCormick's house." He picked up a key that was attached to a metal key ring with a tiny tag dangling on a string with the security code written on it. I refrained from grabbing it. "I thought that maybe you could stay after Leo leaves, and we could sneak over there. Pull a naughty prank on the creep. Get back at him for messing with you."

The look on his face screamed his intentions. He wanted to be alone with me. He did not want to be just friends. Vivian, you were a fool to think that you could control how Wyatt or Leo feels or thinks. You thought you could just make everybody friends by working on a project and that was that. Looking at Wyatt's intense eyes and his willingness to play on my addiction to steal from McCormick, proved he wanted more than friendship. Leo would never agree to breaking into anyone's house, even nasty McCormick, even to win my affections. But Wyatt was wild and without parental guidance. He did what he wanted, when he wanted, and without ramifications. Look at his parties. He never got in trouble. What he clearly wanted was me, and he would risk breaking into a house to please me and be alone with me.

The door opened and Leo walked in. Wyatt quickly put the key back in the top drawer and followed me to the table where there was pizza.

"What's going on?" Leo looked curious at our whispered exchange.

"Oh nothing," I lied—again. "I'm starving." I opened the pizza box and avoided looking at Leo's face. "Let's start brainstorming ideas," I said and shoved a piece of pizza in my mouth.

As Leo and Wyatt began writing down ideas, I tried to listen, but the key and code in that top drawer was like a magnet pulling my attention away. I kept glancing at it as if it was going to run away.

The music was getting louder outside, reminding us that it was getting later and later. Someone poked their head in and yelled, "Yo, Wyatt, come out here. Some girls are getting out of control by the pool."

We followed Wyatt out the door and two girls were dancing on the far side of the pool, taking off their clothes in a drunken strip tease. Everyone was cheering them on. Then, in the crowd of obnoxious teens, stood old man McCormick, leering at the display, with a girl hanging on each side of him. Leo and Wyatt caught my stare.

"Look at that disgusting pig," I spat. "Why would those two girls fawn on him like that?"

Wyatt surprised me by saying, "Girls are all alike. They just want money."

Infuriated, I snapped, "They do NOT! How can you make such a sexist comment?!"

I turned to Leo for support and said, "Do you think that?"

Before Leo could answer, the party took a wild turn with people chanting, 'strip, strip, strip' and Wyatt quickly disappeared to handle a crash coming from the kitchen.

Leo calmly responded, "Yes."

Disgusted by Wyatt and Leo and McCormick and the grotesque display by the pool, I turned around to march off and Leo followed me to the garage door and grabbed my upper arm. I whirled around, yanking my arm away from his grasp dramatically, "WHAT?!"

"Stop acting all self-righteous. You say you hate money. You take from the rich to give to the poor and needy, acting like Robin Hood, but I see how you look at Wyatt. You like him. I can tell. You acted like you hated him at first, but something changed. You started coming over here and hanging out with him. You fell for all this," and Leo lifted his arm towards the grand home. Face it, Viv. Admit it. You like it. You like the mansion and the fancy car. You say you are different, but you are just like them."

Who was this person in front of me? It was like I was staring at a stranger. I didn't recognize him at all. He looked angry and aggressive and insecure, not the Leo I loved.

Wyatt came bursting out the side door, yelling for us to come and help him. Leo looked at me, then at Wyatt's desperate face and ran towards the kitchen door.

Hatred fueled my next move. I turned into the garage and ran to the top drawer of the metal cabinet to get the key and code. I grabbed my backpack and bike and exited, dropping my bike off at the old hiding place in the bushes before bounding up the huge front steps leading to McCormick's front door.

I shoved the key into the dead bolt and tried to turn it, but it wouldn't budge. I pulled the key out and put it back in and jiggled hard. Nothing. The key wasn't working. Suddenly, the door jerked open, and I jumped in shock. McCormick stood there with a teen clinging to his side.

"Ahhh, what do we have here?" he sneered.

I turned to run, and he grabbed my arm so hard I couldn't move. "Did you really think that key would work? When I saw you hanging with the Wilson kid, I changed my locks. Looks like you are just like your mom. You like the fine goods. You like the helicopter rides. The Maserati rides. Don't you? The boys from Lorenzo won't satisfy your luxurious tastes now, will they? You need power. Taking my watch. You are just like every other whore. All you want is money. Well, when you are done fooling around with that child, come to papa. I will give you everything you will ever need."

I wanted to vomit! I wanted to scream! The last thing in the world I wanted was to see that horrid human again. How could they all think I was materialistic? Money was the last thing I wanted or needed. I HATED MONEY! In fact, I wanted the opposite. How could I be so misunderstood? I hated them all! I didn't want a boyfriend now or ever!

"When you are ready for the big leagues, you know where to find me," he let go, turned back to his current conquest, a young girl from the party, and shut the door.

I turned to flee down the steps and passed the limo parked in the circular drive. Impulsively, I pulled the handle of the backseat. It opened. Unzipping my backpack, I grabbed my jar of roaches. I never left the house anymore without my backpack and jar of roaches. Who knew when I would need them. Unscrewing the mesh lid, I unleashed the swarm.

Then I grabbed my bike from the bushes and wheeled away. Away from this horrible night.

Chapter Forty-eight

I rode my bike home with such speed, I nearly got hit twice by cars. Coasting up the driveway, I secured my bike in the garage and flew by my parents' room where the light was on.

My dad yelled, "woa, Viv, come here."

Reluctantly I stopped and turned round. "Yea?"

"Your mom wants to say something."

Mom scribbled on her notepad, 'Are you OK? I'm worried about you.'

I didn't want to talk to Mom right now. Mom was like the girls Leo and Wyatt and McCormick lumped together and called materialistic. I wasn't like her. I was the opposite of her. I liked our little house with its window boxes. I didn't need tons of clothes and shoes. I didn't need a giant house. I. Wasn't. Like. Her.

Leo *was* right about my liking Wyatt. I didn't want to like him, but I did. Not for the reasons Leo thinks. I saw something I recognized in Wyatt. Loneliness. Survival. Independence. All from being left alone. We understood each other in a way Leo would never get. But now, I didn't care what Leo or Wyatt thought of me. I knew I wasn't materialistic. I didn't need to prove it to them.

"I'm fine. Just tired," I said catching my breath.

Mom scribbled, 'Don't forget we are hanging out together tomorrow. Just you and me?'

I looked at her face, soft and serene. Even though she couldn't talk, she looked peaceful and content. Could she have changed? Could she be happy, here, in our little home? Could she be happy without shopping for new clothes?

I looked at Dad lying next to her, eyes smiling as he chimed, "Sounds fun. Your mom is getting stronger, and I will be busy at the job site all day. Then I have bids on two new projects and an AA meeting at 6:00. I haven't been since your mother's accident, and I realize I need it. Then, we are all going to church on Sunday. Together. As a family," Dad gave me a reassuring smile like he knew I knew about his drinking relapse. He wanted me to know he wasn't going to let himself slip and ruin us again.

Dad patted the bed signaling for me to come sit, and I did. They both leaned forward to give me a hug. A hug I didn't realize I needed so badly until their arms were around me. I went limp, as if my bones evaporated, and I began to cry. A quiet cry at first, followed by louder cries. I couldn't stop. They pulled me between them like when I was a little girl and teased, 'sandwich kiss'. I laughed through my sobs.

I heard mom choke out a garbled but audible, "I'm so sorry for everything I have done. I want to spend the rest of my life making it up to you."

Dad whispered, "I am sorry, too, Viv. I am so sorry, and I will go to AA meetings every day if that's what it takes to keep me sober and us together."

I couldn't stop crying.

Chapter Forty-nine

I fell asleep so quickly and deeply that I was startled when I woke in my parents' bed. Dad had already left for work, and Mom was in the kitchen. She emerged holding a tray loaded with breakfast. She walked slowly to the bed, and I realized she wasn't using her cane.

"Thank you, Mom," I said, sitting up.

She set it down, and I took it from her, placing it between us as she rejoined me in bed. She scribbled, 'You were exhausted. How do you feel?'

"Fine," I said, and I did feel fine. Emotionally, I was spent. I didn't have the mental energy to even think about everything that happened last night. All I really cared about was that my parents seemed solid and content. That brought me peace.

After filling up on eggs, bacon, toast and fruit, mom took the tray.

I said, "I can get it." But she shook her head strongly and got up to take everything to the kitchen. I heard her cleaning the dishes and noticed her sketchbook at the end of the bed. Curious, I began flipping through the pages, starting at the beginning. There were sketches of clothes. Pages and pages of dresses. Very good, actually. Then, flowers. Pages and pages of flowers. Flowers in vases. Flowers in fields. Flowers in gardens. Flowers in window boxes. The last half of the sketchbook was filled with flowers.

I looked around the room and spotted my backpack along the wall. I got out of bed and grabbed it, unzipping one of the side pockets for my phone. Dead. Just as well. I got back into bed before mom returned.

Soon, she reemerged. "These are beautiful, Mom." And I meant it.

She smiled and mouthed 'thank-you.'

She sat down, grabbed her small communication notepad, and wrote, 'Leo stopped by looking for you last night. Your dad told him you were safe and sleeping. He said to call him today. Then, another boy came by named Wyatt. He was checking on you, too. We told him you were fine. He wants you to call him today, too.'

She didn't ask me any more questions.

I got up and went to my room to plug in my phone and get my sketchbook. I changed into sweats and went back to Mom, and the two of us just sketched all morning. I hadn't drawn in my notebook in a while. It felt therapeutic.

***

After lunch, mom wrote, 'Let's go visit Sharon.'

Mom wanted to try driving and Sharon's Riches was only a few blocks away, so it would be safe practice. Mom managed to get into the car just fine, and I could see she was getting a lot stronger. When we pulled up to the curb to parallel park, I noticed the beautiful building across the street had finished construction. A coffee house had opened next to a 'make your own pottery' art studio next to a large empty space that said, 'For Lease.'

"Mom, do you want to go paint a vase or something after we say hi to Sharon?"

Mom nodded 'yes' enthusiastically as I opened the door to Sharon's. Sharon saw us and squealed with excitement. Sharon's friend Arnie was standing next to her and came to give me a hug. Sharon and Mr. Cooper had stopped by a few times over the last month to check on us, so mom knew all Sharon had done for me in her absence.

"This is that beautiful young girl I want to come work at Saks with me. And you must be her stunning mother. OMG, you two look like twin sisters!" Arnie's happy disposition was infectious.

"Arnie is helping me plan my wedding. Come in and sit," Sharon ushered us to the two purple velvet chairs.

Sharon modeled her wedding dress for us, a simple white sheath with spaghetti straps that elegantly clung to her figure, and with her milky white skin and long silky black hair, she looked like model. We all oooed and ahhhhed at how beautiful she looked. Sharon then showed us pictures of a stunning white rose bouquet and an arch flanked with breathtaking white hydrangeas. They were getting married at the beach in a few weeks, and we all agreed it was going to be a fabulous event.

"I think we are going to go paint something at the new pottery place," I said.

"That sounds like fun. I love the new coffee house next to it," Sharon added.

"This whole area is jumping with new businesses. A block over is a new interior design center my husband is working at," Arnie theatrically gestured with his hands. "The place is A-MAZ-ing! I will give you a tour of it sometime."

We said our good-byes, and Mom and I walked across the street to the pottery place. When we got inside, the small art studio was filled with unique vases, plates, cups, and figurines. We walked slowly around the room. I knew what I wanted to do. I wanted to recreate the

Picasso plate. I found a blank plate about the size of the original and pulled up a picture of it online. I began selecting paint.

Mom picked out a beautiful vase. She scribbled on her notepad that she wanted to make it for Sharon as a wedding present. I told her that was a great idea.

We spent the rest of the afternoon painting. I loved it. Looking up at mom as she painted white roses on a blue background, I felt like life was getting back to normal, like when I was little. My heart suddenly settled into such complete calmness and contentedness, I was overwhelmed by the unrecognizable feeling, a feeling I wanted to last forever. Forgiving mom suddenly seemed possible.

I looked at my abstract Picasso replica and compared it to the one online. It looked almost identical. One last heist from McCormick to pay all the medical bills HE owed for hurting my mother was justified. Then my family will have no worries, and life will be like this—happy, peaceful moments filled with love.

"Are you all about done?" The owner of the little shop asked.

"Yes," I replied.

"These will take several days to glaze and fire in the kiln. You can pick them up Thursday."

I handed my plate to her. "Lovely," she admired.

Mom was just finishing up, so I made small talk with the owner. "When did you open?"

"It has been about a month, and I've been super busy. This whole area is alive with action! Earlier this morning Conrad McCormick was next door with the leasing agent. He wants to put a McCormick's department store there. I spoke with him myself. He is such an amazing businessman," the lady acted so impressed. "He said he was flying out tomorrow but would be back later in the week to work out the details. Imagine. A McCormick's right next door! That will be great for my business!"

Stunned and speechless, I whipped my head to look at mom. Her hands were shaking. She fidgeted and stood all flustered, picking up her vase and then bobbling it, sending the pottery crashing and shattering on the floor. We all looked, frozen, at the chunks of white roses broken into bits and scattered.

Right then I knew. I knew she remembered everything that happened between Conrad McCormick and her. What mom experienced with that man, I would never completely know, but I knew enough.

That bastard! That predator! He is a grotesque monster! Why won't he leave us alone!? He's ruining my family! How could mom have fallen for him? I HATED HIM!!!

The lady quickly began sweeping up the pottery pieces and said we could come back and do another one at no cost. Mom kept mouthing 'I'm sorry' as tears welled up in her eyes.

Chapter Fifty

Mom could never know that Conrad was stalking me. She wouldn't be able to handle it. I saw the look of sheer terror on her face. I saw her body shake in fright. I saw the tears in her eyes. However vulnerable she was to McCormick's materialistic charms at one time, he meant nothing to her now. More than nothing. He meant fear.

Today, I could tell mom had changed. What happened between McCormick and her was so horrible, she was not the same and probably never will be. Losing her voice, and the abuse and humiliation she suffered at the hands of that psycho, turned her into someone foreign. Today, mom seemed weak, skittish, vulnerable. Not the 'in charge of it all' Mom I knew before she left us. I was not going to upset Mom anymore with news of McCormick following me. That was my secret.

She was sleeping now. It was 5:00 and Dad wouldn't be home for a while. I checked my phone.

Leo left a message: I'm sorry.

Wyatt left a message: You OK?

I didn't know how to respond to either message.

So, I didn't.

I went to my room, laid on my bed and just let my mind fester. Did Leo really think I was materialistic? Was that really what he thought of me? I couldn't believe that to be true. It just wasn't like the Leo I knew. He was just jealous. That had to be it. And Wyatt? He didn't accuse me of being materialistic, just girls in general. That irritated me, too. Because all girls weren't the same, and it wasn't fair that he clumped us all together.

But Leo and Wyatt were the least of my worries. McCormick was my biggest problem, and these mind games he was playing with my family and me were going to stop. Now. I turned the channel in my head to 'Payback Time.' I needed to do something soon. Before that man leased the building across from Sharon's Riches. The idea of him lurking around my world for the rest of our lives sent me over the edge.

Tonight. When dad gets home and goes to sleep, I will get this over with once and for all.

Chapter Fifty-one

I dressed carefully. A black one-piece bathing suit with a beautiful black billowy sundress over it. Wedge sandals. Hair loose and wild.

I had purchased a silver briefcase-like box with a foam-padded interior and metal clasps from Walmart, and it was the perfect size to protect the Picasso plate. When I found it, I was amazed at how light it was. Next, I opened my backpack and placed the case carefully inside and zipped it closed. Then, I gently slid the jar of roaches in an outer zipped cavity of the backpack. Shoving rubber gloves into the dress's deep side pockets and securing my backpack over my shoulders, I crept silently out the side door after everyone was asleep. Quietly, I wheeled my bike out of the garage and peddled towards the beach. Towards McCormick's.

Adrenaline coursed through my veins, sending my heart pumping wildly. All the way there, I rehearsed my actions. Boldly knock on the door. Get invited in by McCormick. Excuse myself to the bathroom. Slip into the office. Swiftly take the plate. Leave my calling card. Then ask to see his boat, and once in the backyard, disappear over the back gate. I didn't have the fake Picasso plate I made to leave as a decoy but didn't care. If he noticed it missing right away, so what?

Next week, I'll have Roy at Priceless Pawn sell the plate. Then I'll go to the police and tell them McCormick has been stalking me. Get a restraining order that keeps him at such a far distance that he won't be allowed to rent the store across from Sharon's. It will be too close to our house. He won't be allowed in my school, on my street, at my beach, or in my town. Portofino is small. So small that I will run him out of my seaside paradise. Goodbye McCormick. I won.

Confidence grew with each brain rehearsal. This must work. This can work. This will work.

There were still cars on the roads, but the closer I got to McCormick's, the quieter and darker the streets became. It wasn't too late. I left at 10 p.m. Late enough for my parents to be in bed, early enough that McCormick would still be awake, hopefully.

I slowed down as I approached Wyatt's mansion. No sign of activity there. I didn't hide my bike. I parked in full view right in front of the large, stone steps of McCormick's. After all, I wasn't doing anything wrong. I was visiting a person. That was it. A friendly visit. A friendly visit making a sick human pay for causing my mom harm. For not leaving us alone.

I pressed the doorbell and heard a loud chime. Swallow Vivian. Take a deep breath. Act cool. I waited. And waited. I pressed it again. And waited. And waited, breathing deeply to calm myself.

I walked around to the side of the house and heard noises and music. Without hesitating, I jumped the rod-ironed gate with effortless skill, even in a dress and sandals. Staying close to the house, I invisibly crept closer to the backyard. Peering around the corner, I saw the activity on the yacht. There was McCormick, drink in his hand, girls giggling and fawning all over him.

I couldn't believe my good fortune. The sliding door to the house was cracked open. No one was paying any attention to the house. I easily walked right in, slipped back to the office, and walked right up to the Picasso plate. Quickly retrieving the gloves from my dress pocket and slipping them on, I gingerly whisked the plate off the shelf, and unzipped my backpack, heart pumping with powerful beats. Leaving the silver case in the backpack, I just unclasped it and slid the plate in it and quickly clasped the case up. Then I unzipped the side pouch and pulled out the jar of roaches.

I was about to unleash them in the office, but suddenly had a better idea. Why draw attention to the office? That is where the Picasso plate will be missing. You don't want that, now, Vivian. You don't want

McCormick to notice anything askew in here. A better idea is to leave them in his bed, as usual. Let him pull back the covers and see roaches everywhere. If he tried to bring an underage girl in here, she would run screaming. Yes, that was a better idea.

Jar in hand, I began to make my way to his bedroom. Then froze. Was that the sliding door? Instant panic made me turn, fumble, and in slow motion, I watched the jar slip from my hands and crash on the floor sending roaches and glass shattering in all directions. The metal lid ponged off the marble floor, bounced, and spun to a slow death.

Instinctively, I ran for the front door, feeling a few roaches taking a ride up my leg. I heard someone approaching faster. I heard a girl shriek. I exited the front door and flew down the steps, slipping off the gloves and shoving them back into my pocket.

My bike?! Gone! Where was my bike?!

When in trouble, head to the sea. I ran across the street to the beach. A heavy fog clung to the dark Gulf waters, and I disappeared into the mist, like a ghost teasing a mortal's eye. Anyone who thought they saw something would doubt my existence.

Under the salty water, I swam rapidly holding my breath, with only a slight drag from my dress and backpack. Finally far enough out to sea, I was confident to emerge and gasped quietly for air. My chest slowed and breathing regained a normal rhythm as I treaded water effortlessly, strengthening up for my final stretch, where I would re-emerge down the shore and walk home.

Just as I started to take casual strokes, a force pulled me under—instantly I knew it was human. Leo following me again? Wyatt joking around? Suddenly, out of the fog and black water surfaced Conrad McCormick!

He reached around my neck and grabbed a fist of my hair, forcing my head back and hissing in my face, "What were you doing in my house? You thieving bitch."

I tried breaking free from his grip, but my head was locked, and I couldn't move. I struggled under the water, my legs thrashing in futile attempt to find ground. Then, miraculously, my toes grazed sand. The sand bar. I was at the sand bar near the pier. I found footing and used that leverage to move my body with McCormick attached onto the solid surface. Within seconds, we were on a ground barrier, water only knee deep. I struggled to break free, but the crazed monster lurched on top of me.

"I'm going to take you right here and then throw you out to sea, leaving you for shark bait—finish you off like I should have done your whore of a mom." His words spewed with spit pellets into my face.

He reached under my dress to discover I had on a one-piece bathing suit. With no easy entry and his sudden lust overtaking him, he let go of my hair to rip off my dress and bathing suit. His mistake. Summoning brute strength, I thrust my knee between his legs with such power, he groaned, and then I pushed his body off me. Leaping into the dark waters on the far side of the sand bar, I disappeared.

Quickly regaining power, he lunged after me. I swam just far enough to get back into deep waters when he grabbed my long hair again. Rage erupted like bottled up molten lava and burst from my body. I wasn't going to let McCormick rape and kill me at sea. My muscled legs instinctively wrapped around the old man's waist, and I jerked him around before taking one giant breath and plummeting under. He was startled and let go of my hair. The strength of my young athletic body was no match for McCormick. He had underestimated my power, my skill, my vengeful hatred that fueled my force. Like an alligator taking down its prey, I circled and circled under water, dragging his body so deep, keeping my legs locked like a vice around his body. Years of swimming had turned me into a skilled aquatic force of nature. He tried to pry free, digging his fingers into my flesh, but like the indestructible roach girl that I am, his attempts to harm me were futile. I didn't even flinch.

Suddenly, in the midst of my vicious defense, Conrad's body weakened and went limp. Was it a tactic to get me to let go? Would he then take me down?

Then I saw something shiny flicker. The Deepsea watch on McCormick's wrist. Impulsively, I let my legs free his body to reach for the watch when he thrashed towards me. I bolted like lightning to the surface.

Once airborne, I took a deep, frantic breath, looking around wildly. Seconds of silence. Not knowing where he was, paralyzed me with fear. Then I saw the water begin to swell on the surface a few feet away. His body emerged and just bobbed lifelessly. Was he faking again? I saw the shiny watch on his outstretched arm. Was he dead? Did I just kill a man? Had I become a monster no better than McCormick—worse? But he attacked me—he had almost killed my mom. I was just defending myself. I watched the waves roll beneath his body, beginning to push him towards shore. The silver watch flickered in the water's blackness. I turned and swam out to the deep sea.

Chapter Fifty-two

I swam and swam and swam. Furiously at first. Then I began to glide. Stroke. Stroke. Glide. Stroke. Stroke. Glide. Stroke. Stroke. Glide.

When I grew weary, I turned over and just floated. My black dress blended with the black sea, giving the illusion that the water and I were one. The wet cotton felt heavy on my body. My backpack, like a lead weight, pulled from under me. I took the backpack off and disrobed, one handed, sending my dress down to the deep dark depths. I felt lighter. I kept ahold of the backpack that held the Picasso plate. Should I let that go, too? The thought of sending $60,000 sinking to the sandy bottom made me tread water a little harder. What was I going to do if it got too heavy?

Before I could think, I heard a stir in the water. My visibility was zero as the misty fog hovered inches over me. Freaked, I looked around. Something was in the water. I sensed it. I felt the tension. There it was again. This wasn't human. Sharks? A fin cut the surface and a bottle nosed dolphin emerged with a small arch, exposing just its slippery backside and blowhole. Then another one. They began to circle me at a distance.

I tried to relax a little, but it was nearly impossible. Maybe talking to them would help, "Hi guys." I said, trying to calm myself. "Are you protecting me? Are you protecting me from sharks? You are good guys, aren't you?" My breathing was quick and erratic.

One made a high-pitched staccato noise as if answering me. I wonder if he or she understood what I said. Was it trying to tell me something? Probably, 'what the heck are you doing out here?'

What *am* I doing out here? What was I thinking? Why did I keep stealing? There were perfectly logical, legal ways to get our family out of our financial problems. But I had this impulsive need to steal, and I used McCormick as my vessel to satisfy this urge. He was bad, so it was OK. Was it OK? He was a creep who lured my mother away from her family with promises of a grand life. He preyed on young girls. He beat my mom and strangled her. Now she can't speak. He was stalking me, coming to my school and donating money, driving up and down my street, leasing a building down the block for one of his stores. He was evil. But did that make it OK for me to take from him? To kill him? Oh God. I killed him. I killed a human. Vivian, you had no choice. He came after you. He was going to kill you. He said so as he grabbed your hair. As he tried to rape you. You were just defending yourself.

Oh, God.... What have I done? Today started so calmly with mom. We sketched all morning, peacefully. We visited Sharon and laughed. We painted pottery. Life felt normal for the first time in so long. I thought, 'this is how things are supposed to be.' Dad went back to AA today and said we were all going to church tomorrow, like a normal family. But when that lady said McCormick was leasing the building next door, and I saw mom shake with fear and her eyes well-up in tears, I snapped. I couldn't let McCormick ruin my family again. Stealing from him had nothing to do with paying off bills at this point, and everything to do with some twisted revenge in my own mind.

Revenge led me to bad choices. Revenge led me here, swimming out to sea. In the dark. Alone. Revenge was going to kill me.

I floated silently. The only sound was the occasional dolphin. I bobbed in the black water, legs peddling to nowhere. Fear so immense, panic so great, body so weak, I couldn't last out here much longer. Defeat was whispering my name.....

I spoke aloud, trying to regain some courage, *'Dear God, what have I done?.................. Help me. Help me make everything right...............Tell me what I should do...................'*

I drifted in more silence, warm, salty water swelling around me, fear trying to swallow me up. I pleaded in a small but desperate voice, *'Please, tell me what I should do?'*

After floating for what seemed like forever, I noticed a break in the fog. Was that a star? Yes. Two, three, dozens of stars. As the night sky cleared for a moment, my thoughts cleared, too, and I knew what to do. It was the only thing I *could* do besides dying out here. Dying was never a consideration for Roach Girl. I had to make it to shore. I had to tell the truth. All of it. The stealing. The struggle with McCormick. All of it. I had to give back the plate. Go to jail. Whatever. I had to come clean and tell the truth. Yes, the truth. The truth is the only way. That was my decision.

My mind was relieved. Time to swim to shore. So, with every last bit of energy, I began to swim and swim and swim. But was I going to shore? I had no idea how far out I was. The fog was still dense in patches, and I couldn't see any lights from the condos. I was in and out of total blackness, except for the occasional star. The waves that once took McCormick's body to shore, moved in all directions around me, leaving me completely confused on which way to go.

Just keep swimming. Stroke. Stroke. Stroke. Glide. Stroke. Stroke. Stroke. Glide.

Chapter Fifty-three

My strong body was giving up on me. My muscles grew weak. I felt them caving within my body and slowly becoming useless. I just floated, trying to reserve energy. Staring straight up, I kept focusing on breathing. The night sky delivered patchy fog with spots of clear black, briefly exposing a few stars here and there. The shore was nowhere in sight. I was feeling faint, and my eyes ached.

My backpack felt like dead weight. I had taken it with me on swims many times with ease, but the struggle with McCormick left me feeling frail. Should I drop the backpack and send $60,000 to the depths of the sea?

Another swoosh…………...swoosh………...let me know my dolphins were still with me. What have I done? I am going to die out here. Was revenge on McCormick worth my life? How could I let my rage for him ruin me? Ruin my family? ……….. *'Mom,' I called out in the blackness. 'I'm sorry. I'm sorry I did such a stupid thing. I want to tell you I love you. I don't hate you. I don't. Not anymore. I forgive you. I forgive you for buying all those fancy clothes and shoes and handbags. I forgive you for wanting the fancy house and car and remodel. I forgive you for leaving us so you could have those things. I don't know that I will ever understand completely why you needed all that stuff, but maybe you were addicted, too. Like dad with alcohol. Maybe shopping filled the hurt and pain of living with an alcoholic. Dad told me to forgive you. That you tried for a long time to help him. I know you were worn out and desperate when you met McCormick. Desperate people do desperate things. You were weak and vulnerable. I get it. It is easy to give up when you are weary.'* I was sobbing now. Sobbing in the middle of nowhere, in the middle of the sea. *'Dad, I love you, too. I'm sorry, daddy. I just thought I could help. I thought I could keep you from relapsing and drinking again. I thought I could help the family stay together……. Leo, I'm sorry. I lied to you when you were so good to me. So kind. I wish I was different. I wish I was a better person, one who deserved your love……Why did I steal things? Why?………. Mom? Did you ask yourself—why do I shop so much?……….. Dad, did you ask yourself—why do I drink so much?'*

Blowing my nose and wiping my face off with salty water, I gained some composure. I don't know why, but talking into the night sky calmed me down, and I stopped crying and drifted some more. Swooooosh....................Swooooooosh..........

'*Mom? Dad? Forgive me? Please? I'm sorry I got myself in such a huge mess. I'm sorry I am about to cause you such pain. You are both dealing with so much, and I am making it worse, not better. Forgive me. Please?*'

Swoooosh................
swooooosh....................swoooooooosh...............
....

My mind began to flicker...weak.... strong....weak....strong....weak....weaker....

I was about to drop the backpack that now felt like a cinder block pulling me under, when I heard a roaring noise from above and a blinding light shining down on me.

Chapter Fifty-four

"Are you sure you are strong enough to talk to the police?" Dad asked, with mom by his side.

Sitting up in the hospital bed, I felt strong and peaceful. Whatever consequence I was about to face was a relief, really. I no longer needed the IV and felt fine. In fact, after meeting with the police, I was being discharged.

Mom and dad were exchanging concerned looks. My calm and peaceful feeling was evaporating, and I asked, "What is going on?"

Before either of them spoke, Leo's dad and a female officer entered. "Hi, Vivian, we have some questions to ask you. Are you feeling up to it?"

"Yes," I replied, eager to get it over with.

"We will be right outside the room if you need us, Viv," dad said as he and mom slipped out.

"Why don't we just start with your account of what happened Saturday night?" The female officer pulled a chair up close and got out a pen and pad. Leo's dad stood on the other side of the hospital bed.

Once I began, the words came easy because I submitted to the truth. Nothing but the truth. And it was liberating. I told them everything. Stealing clothes all summer from McCormick as some sort of twisted revenge for what he did to mom. Stealing and selling the Rolex watch, keeping one, and then McCormick taking it back when he saw me wear it at Lorenzo. McCormick stalking me. My dad drinking again. How I blamed McCormick. How I couldn't stop the need to get back at him. How he was going to lease that store to keep taunting my family, and I thought I would never be rid of him. How I went to his house to take the Picasso plate and then couldn't find my bike, so I ran to the beach and swam out to sea…to escape. But McCormick followed me into the water. We had a struggle. He tried to rape me on the sand bar and said he was going to leave me for shark bait. How he tried ripping off my clothes and grabbing me by the hair. How I took him under. How I saw his body float away. How I panicked and swam further to sea.

Leo's dad stood and listened, and the female officer recorded and wrote everything down.

"Am I going to jail?" I asked matter-of-factly. I had resigned in my head that I would go to jail. I was at peace with it.

"Vivian, you are not going to jail. Our department has been investigating McCormick ever since your mother's near-death encounter. It has been hard because McCormick has buddies in very high places. He gives a LOT of money to political campaigns, but we have seven girls who have come forward claiming he has drugged and raped them. Yes, you did steal from him, but that didn't give him the right to assault you."

"But I killed him. I am not going to go to jail for that?" I asked bewildered.

Leo's dad and the female officer exchanged odd looks. I was suddenly uneasy and sat up straight.

Leo's dad looked confused and said, "Vivian, McCormick isn't dead. You didn't kill him."

"What?" I had a weird mixed feeling of relief and anxiety. I was relieved I didn't kill a person, but I felt sudden fear that he was still out there.

"As the search team went looking for you, we had officers looking for McCormick as well. He managed to slip out of town on his private jet. Do not worry, Vivian. He will not be able to hide forever. We will catch him. We have a warrant out for his arrest. It is just a matter of time before that guy is behind bars."

I didn't know how to feel. I sat there, numb.

"Just one more thing. You said you had a backpack with an expensive Picasso plate in it, correct?" Leo's dad questioned.

"Yes."

"Hmmm. Did you drop it in the ocean?"

"I remember getting weak and thinking about dropping it. I guess I must have," I answered.

The lady officer wrote some more, and Leo's dad said, "That's it for now. Rest and get stronger."

As they walked out of the room, I sharpened my memory and thought hard. I remember Wyatt shouting to put the strap around my waist. I remember being lifted and flying through the air......... I remember touching the straps of my backpack and thinking....I'm going to give it back and tell the truth.

I was about to stop them and tell them of my recollection, but I didn't.

Chapter Fifty-five

I stayed home from school for two weeks. Since Wyatt and I had all but one class together, he brought my schoolwork over every Monday, but I wouldn't see him. Both Leo and Wyatt kept wanting to see me, but I put them off. I needed that time with my parents. Dad had gotten enough work to begin paying off the hospital in regular installments, with plenty left to take care of the home. Mom and I spent days sketching and cooking together. We started a flower garden in the backyard, and I tore up the roach trap.

Sharon and Arnie came over one day when dad was at a job site and entertained Mom and me. Their enthusiasm for life was infectious and needed. Sharon gave us the latest details on the wedding which was in three weeks, and Arnie told us all about how his husband leased the space next to the pottery place for a high-end secondhand furnishings store. Apparently, the super-rich grow tired of their furniture and redecorate as often as common people change clothes. He thought the placement of the store right across from Sharon's designer second-hand clothing boutique was perfect.

No one mentioned that McCormick was supposed to lease that space.

***

Finally, one morning at the kitchen table, Dad said gently, "It's time to get on with life, Vivian," Mom gave me an agreement smile and nod.

I knew they were right, and I couldn't hide forever. Dad continued, "I told Leo and Wyatt to come over today. You need to talk to them. They saved your life."

During my two-week hiatus, the police interviewed me a few more times. During one of the meetings, Leo's dad told me that Leo had followed me that night and swam out to save me but couldn't find me. He called the police and then called Wyatt, who called his dad's pilot, and they immediately went to search for me, along with the coast guard.

Air traffic control confirmed that McCormick escaped to his private island. He had not returned.

What I couldn't figure out was what happened to my backpack and the Picasso plate. I was almost certain I had it when I was lifted into the helicopter, but no one had come forward with it. The police thought I dropped it in the ocean, but I distinctly remember touching the straps on my shoulders when I was air lifted.

***

Shortly after lunch, Leo and Wyatt stood in my living room. I ran to them, hugging Leo first and then Wyatt. Tears welled up in my eyes, and I uttered 'thank you' through a choked voice. The emotions I felt looking at them were overwhelming.

"We have a surprise for you," Wyatt said. "Go get your bathing suit."

I started to object, but then thought, yes. I need to do this.

"We will have her home by supper, Mr. James," Leo said.

Wyatt had traded in the Maserati for a restored green and cream-colored VW van with three surfboards strapped to the top. We climbed in and headed for the beach.

Wyatt knew a remote place far from tourists and new to both Leo and me. I hadn't been in the water since the night with McCormick, and to my surprise, the saltwater felt like a silky warm blanket around my skin. Waves were nonexistent and we ended up lying on top of the surfboards on the still, glass Gulf staring at the bright blue sky and talking.

They filled me in on everything that has been happening at school and how a new corporation was sponsoring the Shark Tank competition.

"Come on. Leo and I want to show you something," Wyatt began paddling to shore and we followed.

I was in the front passenger seat and Leo was behind me, as Wyatt drove closer to his house. Leo sensed I might be tense as we neared McCormick's, so he gently touched my shoulder as if to say, 'Everything will be Ok.'

We got out of the van and went to the garage. Leaning against the wall was my bike.

When Wyatt saw me looking at it, he said, "I found it thrown into the hedge." And he pointed in the direction of my old hiding place. How it got there, no one would really know. Hanging on the handlebars was my backpack. I walked over to it like a dazed-out zombie, reaching for the zipper. Empty. No metal box. No Picasso plate. I turned to look at Wyatt and Leo, confusion etched on my face. Wyatt and Leo just stared at me.

Then Wyatt changed the subject and said, "We filled out the paperwork for the Shark Tank competition and wrote your name down to be on our team. We have an idea. Dolphins were circling you, protecting you from nearby sharks the night of your accident. We did some research on dolphin behavior."

Leo continued, "Dolphins work in pods to take down sharks. Scientists have discovered that Orcas—who are in the dolphin family—make a sound that sends sharks away in fear."

Wyatt opened a sketchbook with a necklace design.

"You press the whistle when you are in the water and an orca sound is sent through the sea, saving a person from any looming sharks," said Leo.

I stared at both of them, side-by-side, so handsome. Wyatt, my Nordic Cherokee adventurer and Leo, my modern Moses saint.

"I love it," I said.

We talked and laughed, made smoothies, and hung by the pool. Finally, I told them I better go. Wyatt said, "I'll throw your bike in the van and drive you home."

"No, I want to ride it," I said, walking to the garage, emerging with my bike, empty backpack strapped on my back.

"See you guys Monday." And I cruised away with the warm late afternoon breeze in my face, wondering what exactly happened to the Picasso plate. Maybe the zipper opened, and it fell out. Probably laying on the ocean floor.

Chapter Fifty-six

Sharon and Mr. Cooper were married October 10th at Lancing Park on the Gulf of Mexico at sunset. Close friends and family attended. The reception was held at Leo's house, where they first met.

Wyatt chauffeured the bride and groom, my parents, and Leo and me from the wedding to the Lamont's for the party. Laughter filled the van. As we turned the corner on our street, the road was blocked off thanks to the Portofino police connection. We bypassed the barrier and pulled up to the sounds of Leo's uncle's band jamming in the backyard. The smell of barbeque filled the air. Twinkle lights draped the streets and backyard. The night was magical.

We danced to mostly 80s music per the bride and groom, but in the midst of the glorious evening, dad went to the band and whispered something to Leo's uncle, and Leo's uncle nodded. The band launched into a classic Fleetwood Mac song, 'Don't Stop'. Soon everyone was singing the lyrics and dancing wildly on the dance floor.

Don't stop thinking about tomorrow
Don't stop, it'll soon be here

It'll be better than before
Yesterday's gone, yesterday's gone
Why not think about times to come?
And not about the things that you've done
If your life was bad to you
Just think what tomorrow will do
Don't stop thinking about tomorrow
Don't stop, it'll soon be here
It'll be better than before
Yesterday's gone, yesterday's gone

Wyatt had become a fixture at the Lamont's house ever since my incident. He had replaced his Friday night wild parties for the fun family affairs at the little yellow house with twinkle lights and laughter. I could tell by the way Wyatt was twirling Leo's mom on the dance floor that he had found his people, much like I found peace here when my parents deserted me.

Peace. Would I ever find complete peace? On the outside everything seemed in order now. But I was going to have to live with the fact that McCormick was still out there. Leo's dad assured me that he would be going to jail once he returned to the states. With all his connections, I had a hard time completely believing he would truly go to jail, and if he did, it was the incident with me that put the final nail in his prison coffin. Sure, other girls were waiting to tell their stories about McCormick, but it was ultimately me and my mom who would send him to his fate. And McCormick wouldn't forget it.

I knew I would have to face him at some point in court. I knew I was going to have to summon up Roach Girl strength to do one last battle with that monster. I knew he would not go down without a fight. No, peace was a luxury I had to go without.

Maybe peace alludes most people. I thought mom always seemed to have it together, but one day she just left, chasing peace in a department store. Dad, a once respected doctor, chased peace in a wine box. I was chasing peace stealing from people I thought had too much.

Maybe I needed to stop chasing it. Just sit still. Let it come to me.

Leo grabbed my hand and pulled me out of my reverie and onto the dance floor. He twirled me around and then pulled me close. I stopped. He stopped. We both melted into each other. He kissed the top of my head as we clung together in a peaceful embrace.

Chapter Fifty-seven

McCormick was arrested at the Portofino airport while trying to return to Florida on Christmas Day. He was denied bail and would remain behind bars until his trial. Even though I knew it was going to be hard facing that man in court, I was relieved it was about to come to an end.

Two days after his arrest, I came home from school and saw a package sitting at the door. In bold black marker was written, "VIVIAN." No postage. No return address. I whisked it up and slipped into my room, undetected by mom or dad. I carefully opened the box and stared in disbelief.

The metal case. I unsnapped the clasps. The Picasso Plate. I turned it over and over, examining every inch in complete shock. Not a chip on it. A chill bolted through my body, and I quickly peeked out the blinds to see if anyone was there. Not knowing what to do or who to tell, I decided to hide the plate under a hardwood plank on the floor in my closet with books stacked on top. I sat carefully on my bed with my back rigidly straight, staring at the now closed closet door. Breathe, Vivian. Breathe.

I closed my eyes and took in two long inhales and exhales, trying to calm my nerves. I should tell mom and dad. I should tell Leo. Wyatt. Mr. Lamont. I should tell someone. But I was paralyzed. I should tell someone. But I didn't know who. I should tell someone. But I decided to tell no one. For now.

***

I was preoccupied all week. Convinced McCormick had sent a calling card, I couldn't make out why. Was he trying to buy my silence? Who did he have deliver the package if he was in jail? Every day on my way home from school, I constantly looked over my shoulder, wondering who might be doing McCormick's dirty work. Paranoia invaded my brain. I should tell someone. I knew I should. It was the rational thing to do. But for some reason, I couldn't. I don't know why. I just needed to think.

My mind began going down the rabbit hole of fear. What if McCormick hired someone to stalk me? Kidnap me? Kill me? Kill my mom, my dad? Stop it. Stop it, Vivian. You are not going to let him intimidate you. I needed to get rid of the Picasso plate. Get it out of my life. I needed to sell it. Give the money away. That would make me feel better. I knew I should turn it over to the police, but I couldn't. The urge to sell it pulsed rapidly through my veins.

A trip to see Roy at the Priceless Pawn was my instinctive Roach Girl reaction. I moved the stack of books and pulled up the plank, carefully lifting the Picasso plate from its hiding place. Staring at the work of art, I thought for a moment. I wanted to sell it, but something told me to wait. Wait a little bit longer. Wait until the trial is over. As I continued to stare, I wondered, *'How did McCormick get the plate? I had it in my backpack when we fought in the water. How could he have gotten it without me knowing? Was I too obsessed with survival that I didn't know he had taken it out of my bag?'* I recreated the horrible night in my head, step by step. I just don't remember him reaching behind me and unzipping my bag. In fact, he couldn't have done that. After I watched him drift away, I remember how heavy the backpack was. I remember wanting to drop it, more than once.

Leo was on the beach looking for me that night. He tried to swim out and save me. Could the metal case have fallen out and he found it on the shore? Maybe he mailed it to me? Wyatt rescued me with the helicopter. Could he have taken the plate out before hanging my backpack on the handlebars of my bike? Both scenarios were possible, but what would Leo and Wyatt's motive be in sending me a mysterious package? Why wouldn't they just give me the plate? Don't be ridiculous. If Leo or Wyatt found the plate, they would just hand it over to me or the police.

It had to be McCormick. Maybe the case fell out right before I was air lifted and drifted to shore, and McCormick was still around and found it then. That was possible. For now, I will just keep the plate. No pawn shop sale yet. I had to think this through some more, so I carefully placed the plate back under the plank. But the desire to sell it and give the money to charity was so overwhelmingly powerful, I knew that Roy would be getting a visit soon.

Afterward

In the months after McCormick's arrest, a media circus erupted. Young girls began coming forward of twisted tails about McCormick. Whispered rumors circulated about powerful people on private planes frequenting his private island paradise.

One report suggested McCormick had a little black book with names so powerful, McCormick could make a deal with authorities for a lesser sentencing.

Then, one week before the trial was about to begin, McCormick was found hung to death in his cell. Suicide they said. I was in complete shock. I couldn't help but feel relieved. The monster was dead. I wouldn't have to testify. Mom wouldn't have to testify. I would stop being stalked. I could walk home without looking over my shoulder. I could sleep at night.

But suicide? That did not seem like McCormick. He was narcissistic. He was arrogant. He felt above the law. He was a dominant fighter, a person who had to win at all costs, a pig who thought he was always right. No. Suicide was not how that man would go down. I just couldn't believe that.

And apparently, some of the press agreed. New rumors began of a murder cover-up. Rumors of guards being paid off. Rumors that McCormick knew too much about too many powerful people. But, eventually, in the weeks and months that followed, like the rising hot sun beating down on an early morning fog, the rumors dissipated. And people stopped talking about Conrad McCormick.

Life went back to normal. Leo, Wyatt, and I dove into our Shark Tank project. We ended up winning the school, county, and state competitions, each of us earning a scholarship to a state university. Leo would start at the University of Florida in the fall, but Wyatt and I had two more years of high school.

Wyatt helped me set up a private account on Ebay, and together, we sold the Picasso plate for $63,333. Getting the plate out of my life was a relief. Giving the money to charity gave me such euphoria. I couldn't explain what it felt like to take money from rich monsters and give it to a good cause. This compulsion was an addiction so powerful; I was not sure I could ever stop. And the private donation to Sharon's charity, Harmony House, that helped victims of the sex trade, seemed justified. But I made Wyatt promise to never tell Leo. Little lies to Leo, again.

Leo. God I was going to miss Leo. In fact, I didn't know how I was going to exist without his constant presence in my life. But summer was about to begin, and I wanted to make this summer magical and not think about Leo leaving for college. I wanted a summer Leo and I would never forget. A romantic summer. A summer as boyfriend and girlfriend—not just friends. A summer of warm Gulf swims, soft, wet kisses, and slow walks on the beach. A summer with no McCormick, no drama, no worries. Just a fun, relaxing, peaceful summer.

***

Then, on the last day of school, when all I could think about was meeting Leo for a sunset walk on the beach, another package arrived on my doorstep. I walked up the path leading to my house with an alarming tightness in my chest. No return address. No postage. 'VIVIAN' was written in black marker just like the other Picasso plate package. Fear grabbed my throat, strangling my ability to breathe. I glanced over both shoulders, in complete shock. McCormick was dead. I thought this ordeal was over. What was going on? Settle down. Settle down. Maybe it was just a gift from Wyatt or Leo. Maybe the lettering wasn't quite the same.

Maybe I was overreacting. Quickly, I scooped up the mystery package and flew to my room.

I opened it.

The Deepsea watch.

I slowly pulled the beautiful silver work of art out of the box. It felt heavy in my hand. I lightly ran my thumb over the glass and along the smooth metal links, staring at the deep, vibrant blue face.

What was going on?

The Deepsea Rolex watch had me hypnotized, and I couldn't stop staring at the rich blue face, running my thumb over the glass and down the cold, metal links again.

Royal blue.

ROLEX.

Crown.

Midnight blue.

DEEPSEA.

SEA-DWELLER.

Mesmerized, I circled my index finger around and around the black and silver dial, feeling each carved notch.

Then, with a sudden urge I couldn't control, I slipped it on.

About the Author

G. Keller is a middle school English teacher. She is married and has two children, two cats, and a dog. When she is not grading papers or spending time with her family, she loves to read, watch The Great British Bake-Off, binge watch a great series, take long walks thinking up stories, and writing, of course.

About the Artist

Janelle Bell-Martin is a freelance illustrator working on book illustration, collectible designs, animation final line art and painting.

Coming soon....

G. Keller and the cover artist, Janelle Bell-Martin, have teamed up to bring you the graphic novel version of the Roach Girl origin trilogy. Book one is due January 2026.

Roach Girl the wilson trilogy is coming out fall 2026.